"Don't you have anything better to do than follow me around?" Megan snapped. *"I don't need a watchdog."*

Caleb raised an eyebrow. "How about a friend?"

"You're not my friend. We both know that. Look, Agent Davis, I know the drill. I've watched enough television to know that you have to consider me a suspect. I have no problem with that. Take my DNA, my fingerprints, whatever. But please hurry, so you can quickly rule me out and focus on finding my son...."

Her chin wobbled a little and she seemed to be fighting for control. It was too much for him, more than he could handle after the dramatic emotions of the day. With a sigh he reached for her and pulled her into his arms. She was perfect there. Soft and womanly, all the things he had been telling himself he could manage without. Her arms slid around his waist, and she rested her head against his chest. Something hard and cold inside him seemed to crack apart, leaving only sweet, healing peace.

**Start off the New Year right—
with four heart-pounding romances from
Silhouette Intimate Moments!**

- Carla Cassidy's WILD WEST BODYGUARDS miniseries continues with *The Bodyguard's Return* (#1447).

- RaeAnne Thayne's *High-Risk Affair* (#1448) is a no-risk buy—we guarantee you'll love it!

- *Special Agent's Seduction* (#1449), the latest in Lyn Stone's SPECIAL OPS miniseries, is sure to please.

- Linda Conrad's NIGHT GUARDIANS keeps going strong with *Shadow Hunter* (#1450).

And starting next month, Silhouette Intimate Moments will have a new name,

Silhouette Romantic Suspense.

Four passionate romantic suspense novels each and every month.

Don't miss a single one!

RaeAnne Thayne

HIGH-RISK AFFAIR

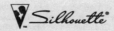

INTIMATE MOMENTS™

Published by Silhouette Books

America's Publisher of Contemporary Romance

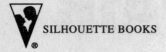 SILHOUETTE BOOKS

ISBN-13: 978-0-373-27518-2
ISBN-10:   0-373-27518-8

HIGH-RISK AFFAIR

Copyright © 2007 by RaeAnne Thayne

Visit Silhouette Books at www.eHarlequin.com

Printed in U.S.A.

RAEANNE THAYNE

lives in a graceful old Victorian nestled in the rugged mountains of northern Utah, along with her husband and two young children. Her books have won numerous honors, including several readers' choice awards and a RITA® Award nomination by the Romance Writers of America. RaeAnne loves to hear from readers. She can be reached through her Web site at www.raeannethayne.com or at P.O. Box 6682, North Logan, UT 84341.

Prologue

Being a special operative was hard, dangerous work but he wasn't afraid to sacrifice for his country.

On his belly in the dirt, pitch-black darkness pressing in on all sides, Cameron Vance adjusted his night vision goggles and tried his best to get his bearings.

The goggles didn't really work well here in the deep mining tunnels and he could barely see where he was going, but he knew he'd been in this part before. He recognized the rusted old mine cart and the fork in the tunnel. He pulled out the small penlight and found the small white arrow he'd drawn with chalk on an earlier trip to point the way out.

By the muted sounds he could hear ahead, he knew he was close to his mission objective—infiltrating a hideout full of Tangos and then taking them down.

They weren't supposed to be there. For the last week,

he had seen lights flickering up here on the mountain where there shouldn't be any. Finally a few nights earlier, he decided he would have to investigate. It wouldn't be easy. He would have to plan an elaborate deception, a daring escape, but he knew he had no choice.

It was his duty and obligation as a loyal soldier to look out for his country's interests.

He had a cover to protect, though, and knew he couldn't just come and go as he pleased. Finally, when he was sure everyone was asleep, he managed to slip out the window and climb carefully down. He had done it before, but those other times had just been practice. This was for real.

No one had detected his escape. He'd made sure of that. No one could have seen him leave the house or witnessed his careful hike up the mountain, his way lit only by the moonlight and his memory.

He moved to the fork in the tunnel, fueled by the adrenaline pumping through him and the deep certainty that what he did here would make the world a better place.

Others might find the heavy darkness inside the mine shaft a little scary. He knew plenty of guys who probably wouldn't have the nerve to come in here. But he was a Navy SEAL, a trained fighting machine, and he wasn't afraid of anything.

As he headed down the shaft, the light grew brighter and his goggles worked much better, casting a greenish glow on everything. He knew right where the Tangos were hiding—the large chamber he had found in an earlier exploration. It would be a perfect staging spot for whatever evil the terrorists might be planning.

It smelled strange here, something harsh and burning.

He hadn't remembered that before. Were they planning some kind of chemical attack? he wondered.

With renewed determination, he moved slowly toward the light, his heart pounding and blood pulsing through him.

He crawled the last fifteen yards on his belly, ignoring the dank stench and the rocks that scraped his skin.

The shaft sloped down into the large chamber, perhaps twenty feet across. He didn't have the best vantage point from up here, but Cameron didn't dare inch closer for fear they might see him.

He could hear them clearly enough, anyway.

"I don't see the problem here," one said, his voice sharp and angry. "I kept my part of the deal. I've been cooking my ass off for two weeks, working in this tomb here. I'm doing all the work and I deserve a hell of a lot more than some lousy quarter cut."

Cameron frowned. Cooking what?

"You're getting your fair share. Who's taking all the risks? I'm the one out there setting up all the deals, working all the angles. I got the ammonia, I made the Mexican connections. Without me, you'd still be in your *Beavis and Butt-Head* lab cooking your little nickel bags."

"And without me all you'd have would be a bunch of worthless chemicals."

"You really think you're so indispensable?"

The older-sounding man's voice was low and sent a chill down Cameron's spine as he crouched in the dirt. That voice seemed familiar, he thought. Where had he heard it before?

"I found this place for you, didn't I? Nobody's ever going to find this lab here. It's perfect. And you have nothing to complain about with the quality of my product. Pure ice, man."

The other man's laugh sounded rough. "Hate to break it to you, Wally, but good cooks are thick on the ground. Anybody who can follow a recipe can do it. Hell, my aunt Mabel could do it. And she might not have the very unfortunate habit of sampling the merchandise."

"Yeah? Well, why don't you just go drag your aunt Mabel in here to finish this batch? I'm out of here. And maybe I'll just drop a bug in the Mexicans' ears about your double-dealing? I doubt they'll be crazy to know you've promised the same shipment to two different parties."

A long silence filled the mine and Cameron thought about inching forward for a better look at what was going on, but he decided he would be wise to stay put for now.

"Surprised you, didn't I?" the one named Wally said after a minute. "You didn't think I knew about your little side deal."

Cameron listened to their argument with mounting confusion. They didn't sound like terrorists. What were they talking about? Whatever it was, he thought it would probably be best if he sneaked back out and contacted local authorities. He started to inch down the way he had come, but he'd only gone a few feet when he dislodged a rock. It went rolling down the slope and thudded off the bottom. He could swear his heartbeat sounded like thunder.

"What was that?" A flashlight beamed in his direction, but Cameron slid farther down the incline to avoid the light.

"Probably a rat," Wally said. "The place is lousy with them."

"I'm beginning to figure that out," the other one said in a strange, hard-sounding voice.

Cameron started to slip farther down the slope, intending to make his way back carefully when he heard a strangled cry from the chamber.

"What the hell is this?"

"You're the smart one. You tell me."

"What, you going to shoot me now?" Wally's voice was filled with a panic Cameron suddenly shared. "Come on, man. Put it away. Twenty-five percent of the cut is fine. I was just dicking around with you."

"That's your mistake," the other man said. "I never had much of a sense of humor."

Suddenly Cam heard a loud bang and then a scream that was cut off abruptly by another bang.

He gasped and instinctively scrambled down the slope, forgetting all about stealth and making far more noise than a good Navy SEAL should.

"Who's there? Anybody there?"

So much for concealing his presence. He groaned to himself, his stomach in knots. He'd blown it, big-time. He could hear the killer making his way up the incline toward him. He had to hide. He couldn't make it to the entrance without exposing his location.

Another shaft led off to the left, but he'd never gone that way and didn't know what he might encounter. He had no choice, though. The man had already killed once. Somehow Cam knew he wouldn't think twice about doing it again.

He made his way cautiously down the tunnel, careful to make as little noise as possible until he was far enough away that he thought it would be safe to run. He moved as fast as he could, until the night vision goggles were useless and the batteries had faded.

He slid down the side of the tunnel wall into the dirt, his breathing ragged and his heart still racing. He couldn't think like a Navy SEAL now, on a secret mission to save the world from the bad guys.

For now, he forgot all about his dad, about terrorists, about pretending to be something brave and heroic.

As he stared through the blackness, he could only be what he was—a scared nine-year-old boy who suddenly wanted his mom.

Chapter 1

2:00 a.m.

Megan Vance arose with a jerk, not sure whether the echo of screams in her ears had been real or imaginary.

Fear knotted her insides, every muscle was contracted, and her breathing came harsh and fast. For one wild, panicky moment she was consumed by a single overwhelming need—to check on her children.

She listened intently but heard nothing except the summer rain clicking against the glass of her bedroom window.

After a moment, she sagged back to the pillow, embarrassed at herself. It was only a nightmare, nothing to send her into a panic. She forced herself to relax her muscles one by one and deliberately moderated her ragged breathing until it was slow and even.

She hadn't had one of those in a while. Though already the details had mercifully faded and she couldn't remember what had left her so terrified, she knew by the sick feeling still lingering in her stomach it must have been a bad one.

She sat up, scrubbing at her face while the last tendrils of the nightmare uncoiled from around her chest. After Rick had died, she used to have them nearly every night—gruesome, twisted journeys through her subconscious, full of monsters and demons.

She could remember a few of the more vivid dreams and they usually involved the horrible deaths of everyone she knew and loved.

Little wonder, she supposed. She had already lost so much. The roll call of people she had loved and lost seemed to grow longer all the time. Her mother—cancer when Megan was twelve. Her father—a cop killed in the line of duty a year later. Her baby brother Kevin—a New York City firefighter killed on 9/11 in Tower One.

And Rick.

Last month had marked two years since her husband's death. She wondered when she would stop expecting his phone call in the middle of the night, telling her his SEAL team had been called up to some trouble spot or another.

I'll be back soon, babe. Love you.

Oh, how she had dreaded those phone calls.

She had lost much but not everything. She still had Cam and Hailey, the joys of her life.

She rolled over onto her back and thought about them. Her children. Hailey, funny and sweet and girlie but with a tough streak that always took Megan by surprise. And Cameron, smart and stubborn and coura-geous even when he had to endure things no child should have to face.

They had saved her these last two years. The normal routine of mothering them—the car pools and soccer games and doctor's appointments—had taken the wild edge off her grief and given her something else besides herself to focus on.

She sighed, praying again that moving them away from San Diego to the wilds of Utah had been the right decision for all of them. Her children needed family. *She* needed family and a support system, and her sister Molly was all she had left.

Moving closer to her and her noisy brood and strong, kind husband had seemed like a stroke of genius, in theory. Her job as a CPA was mobile, and she could find work anywhere helping small businesses with their payroll and accounting.

Rick used to tease her about her obsession with num-bers. To a man who jumped out of airplanes and climbed every mountain he could find, she supposed it was an obsession. But Megan enjoyed what she did and was good at it.

In only the few short months they had been in Moose Springs, she had already built up a nice client list. Ev-erything seemed to be working out just as she hoped.

Still, Megan couldn't help worrying. Oh, Hailey seemed to be adapting all right, but Cameron had been angry about leaving behind all his friends, his soccer team, the climbing wall Rick had built for the children inside their San Diego home.

Most of all, he hadn't wanted to leave his dad's SEAL

team members, who had taken the boy under their considerable wing after they had lost one of their own.

He would adjust, she told herself again. Lately he seemed to enjoy exploring the foothills around their house and once school started in a few weeks he would make new friends, find a new soccer team, develop new interests.

The wind rattled raindrops against the glass again and Megan sat up, reaching for her robe. She would just peek in on them. That didn't make her a neurotic mother, just a loving one.

She automatically went to Cameron's room first. His seizures tended to hit when he was awake but he'd had a few in his sleep.

In the glow of the night-light shaped like a soccer ball, she could see his form under the covers, the blankets over his head as he preferred.

She stood for a moment looking around the room. She always found it a little painful to see this shrine to his father's memory. Navy recruiting posters covered all the walls and Cam had hung one of Rick's SEAL T-shirts in a place of honor, along with his father's picture and the many medals he'd been awarded, both before the Afghanistan helicopter crash that killed him and posthumously.

Her sister thought Megan shouldn't encourage his obsession with all things military. With his epilepsy, he could never be able to serve in any branch of the service, let alone a physically demanding special forces unit like the SEALs.

But Megan hadn't the heart to take this away from him, not when it was the only way he knew to connect with the father he had idolized.

With one more look at the bed, she closed the door and walked across the hall to check on Hailey.

Unlike her brother, who liked to sleep like a potato bug all curled up under his covers, six-year-old Hailey sprawled across her bed, her quilt thrown off and her pink ruffly nightgown riding up to her knees.

Her bedroom was like her—pink and girlie, with a cupboard full of Barbies and her American Girl doll on the nightstand, standing guard over the only discordant element in the room, Hailey's pet rat Daisy.

The rat blinked at her, turned around once in her cage, and went back to sleep. Megan shuddered. She hated the darn thing and had lobbied hard to leave her behind with a classmate back in San Diego, but Hailey wouldn't be swayed.

She tucked the blanket back up over her daughter, knowing it would be down again in a few moments, then left Hailey's door ajar.

In the hallway, she contemplated going back to bed but she wasn't at all sleepy. With her mind racing now, she knew trying to sleep would be futile for some time.

She would go down and make some tea, she decided, and perhaps grab her knitting bag and knit a few rows on her latest project to calm herself and relax enough to go back to sleep.

She walked down the stairs and out of habit checked the dead bolt and the security system.

She started for the kitchen then paused, something niggling at her. The nightmare she couldn't even remember now had left her unsettled, uneasy. She frowned and turned around, some motherly instinct guiding her back up the stairs to Cameron's room.

She had learned not to question that intuition. More than once she had been guided to drop whatever she was doing to search for him, only to find him in the grips of a seizure.

His epilepsy had been under control with medication for some time and he had been sleeping soundly five minutes ago, but she knew that could change in an instant.

She studied the shape on the bed under that Army green blanket. Something was off. Though she hated to wake him, she reached for the blanket and tugged it down, then felt her whole world turn ice-cold.

Instead of Cameron's tousled blond hair and freckled nose, she found a rolled-up sweatshirt. She yanked the blanket off and gasped at the pillows stuffed there to approximate a nine-year-old boy's shape.

Her son was gone!

4:45 a.m.

"You sure you're up to this again so soon? I can find somebody else."

FBI Special Agent Cale Davis turned off his electric razor and flipped up the lighted visor mirror of the agency SUV. "I'm good," he answered. "I'm glad you called me."

His partner frowned at Cale's assured tone as he drove through the predawn darkness through a sparsely populated region of Utah.

"I should have tried a little harder and found someone else." Gage McKinnon gave a heavy sigh. "Allie's going to skin me alive when she finds out I called you. You only had two weeks off and you need at least double that after what happened."

"Leave it, McKinnon. I'm fine. Two weeks was more than enough."

Gage looked as if he wanted to argue, but he didn't, much to Cale's relief. He would prefer talking about anything else but his last case and its horrible ending.

"What else can you tell me about this missing kid?" he said to turn the subject.

The SUV's headlights illuminated a carved and painted wooden sign for Moose Springs, population three hundred and eleven. Probably some overachieving Boy Scout's Eagle project, he thought.

The town was about an hour east of Salt Lake City, bordering the Uinta National Forest. He'd been here only once before in an official capacity, in a case involving a good friend, Mason Keller. Unofficially, he had been here many times. Mason and his wife Jane lived on a small ranch nearby and the town had always struck him as clean and friendly. *Mayberry R.F.D.* in a cowboy hat.

He didn't want to think something dark and sinister might lurk here. Yet when the FBI called out its Crimes Against Children unit, chances were good all was not as picture-perfect as he wanted to believe here in this quiet community.

"Cameron Vance, nine years old," Gage answered him after a moment. "Father, Rick Vance, killed in action in Afghanistan. Mother Megan, thirty-two, works out of the home as an accountant. Mom puts the boy to bed at usual time. Goes in to check on him around two and finds him gone, a blanket rolled up to make the casual observer think he's sleeping away. There was no sign of forced entry and the alarm system was engaged and undisturbed, but there was also no obvious escape route either from the second-story window. No dangling bedsheets, no convenient awning. It's fifteen feet to the ground, heck of a leap for a nine-year-old kid."

Not if the kid was a limber little monkey like Charlie Betran, Mason and Jane's adopted son, Cale thought.

"What compelled the mother to check on him? Does he make a habit of wandering?"

"According to initial reports from local authorities, Megan Vance said she had a nightmare around that time and checked both children out of habit."

"Any idea what time he disappeared?"

"We've got a four-hour window between ten when Mrs. Vance checked on him before going to bed and two when she awoke again."

"She didn't hear any suspicious noises?"

"Nothing, just the wind." McKinnon studied the GPS coordinates on the dashboard unit, then turned at the next street and headed out of town again before going on with his narrative. "After she finds him missing, the mother spends a little time looking around the house and yard, then calls local authorities around oh-three-hundred, who immediately issue an Amber Alert and call us."

"What makes anybody think a crime has been committed here? Sounds like the kid just sneaked out. It seems a little early in the game for Amber Alerts and calling in the FBI."

"You'd think," Gage said, "but this has the potential to be a high-profile case and I think the local authorities want to make sure all their bases are covered from the beginning. They're running it as a crime scene until they have evidence that it's not."

Another high-profile case. Great. Cale closed his eyes. The image of two pretty little girls with dark curls instantly burned behind his eyelids and he jerked them open again.

He wasn't sure he had the stomach for this again.

"I'm not seeing it from the information you've given me. What makes this case stand out?"

"Besides the fact that his father was a national hero who died serving his country, the kid has epilepsy. There's an urgency here because the mother's terrified he's had a seizure somewhere."

If anyone could find the boy, Gage was the man. His partner was known as The Bloodhound and he specialized in missing children cases. He had an uncanny knack for finding lost kids.

Cale had often wondered if his partner's own history gave him some kind of sixth sense, some inner eye that guided his actions.

On the other hand, he had his own grim history and his past usually seemed more of a hindrance than a help.

"What do you see as our role here?"

"Purely advisory at this point, providing assistance to the local investigators as needed."

Judging by the bright flash of emergency vehicles against the night sky, they were approaching the boy's house. Gage climbed a slight grade and the whole chaotic scene stretched ahead of them.

In the strobing glow from a dozen cop cars and search and rescue vehicles, Cale saw the house was a two-story log structure with a steeply pitched gable on one end and a wide porch along the front.

A basketball standard hung from the detached garage, and two bikes were propped against the porch.

Most of the vehicles were parked some distance from

the house. He saw this as a good sign that local authorities had been careful to protect the scene as much as possible.

Gage pulled in next to a van with the logo of one of the local TV stations emblazoned on the side. Then the two of them headed for the house.

They showed their badges to the uniform cop at the door. Once inside, Cale's gaze was instinctively drawn to a woman on the couch. Though she was surrounded by a bevy of uniformed personnel, somehow she seemed alone in the room.

The mother. It had to be. She was small and red-haired, with a wispy haircut and delicate features that just now looked ravaged.

He could fill a chapel with the faces of all the grieving mothers he'd had to face in his career, but somehow each one managed to score his heart anyway.

He forced himself to turn away from her raw devastation, focusing instead on a dark-haired, muscular man who stood in the center of the action, towering above everyone else.

The Moose Springs sheriff was no stranger to him, and it looked as if Daniel Galvez had the situation well in hand.

Galvez made eye contact with him briefly, then broke off his conversation with the officer and headed in their direction, his big hand outstretched.

"Davis! Sorry I had to drag you boys from the FBI down here already, but we don't want to miss anything on this one."

"No problem," Cale said. "This is my partner, Gage McKinnon."

The two men shook hands. "I know you don't have time to babysit us," Gage began, "but can you just spare a minute to bring us up to speed on the search so far?"

Galvez shook his head. "We're baffled. The kid seems to have vanished. At this point, we haven't turned up any signs that anyone else was involved but we just don't know."

"What about friends? Could he have snuck out to meet up with someone?"

"He doesn't have many. His cousins, mostly. Megan and the kids only moved to town a few months ago."

"What about search dogs?"

"They're on their way. They've been in Wyoming looking for a lost hiker but should be here by the time the sun comes up, when we can mount a full-scale search of the surrounding mountains."

"What about closer to home?" Cale said with a meaningful look at the mother.

Galvez suddenly looked tired. "I just don't know. My gut's saying no. Like I said, the family has only been here a few months, but as far as I can tell there's nothing in their background to point any fingers to the mother. From all accounts, Megan Vance is a devoted mother who's had a rough road."

She certainly looked devastated by her son's disappearance, Cale thought with another glance at the woman on the couch. But he knew outward appearances could sometimes hide rotten insides.

"You said they've only been here a few months," he said. "Where were they before they moved?"

"San Diego."

"Why the move?"

"Mrs. Vance's sister lives about a half mile down the road with her husband and four children," he answered. "Molly and Scott Randall. I gather Mrs. Vance wanted to be closer to family. It would be tough raising two kids by yourself."

Sometimes the strain of twenty-four-hour single parenting could make even the most seemingly devoted parent crack. Cale had seen it before and he wasn't willing to rule anything out yet.

"I'm assuming you want to talk to Megan Vance," Galvez said.

No. He wanted to stay as far as possible from that traumatized-looking woman on the couch. But he knew his job.

"Definitely."

His partner gave him a careful look. His shoulder ached. Cale wondered how long it would be before everybody stopped looking at him as if he were a big bundle of unstable plastic explosives just waiting for an ignition source.

He returned Gage's scrutiny with cool regard, and after a moment the other agent nodded.

"You run the mother. I'll go talk to the crime scene unit and see if they've come up with anything," McKinnon said.

He headed up the stairs and Cale turned toward the mother. Up close, Megan Vance looked even more fragile. Breakable, like an antique pitcher teetering on the edge of a shelf.

She clasped her hands tightly together on her lap, but he could see even that couldn't still their trembling. Her whole body shook, he saw as he approached. Not constantly, but every few seconds, a shiver would rack her slight frame.

"Mrs. Vance, I'm Special Agent Caleb Davis with the Salt Lake office of the Federal Bureau of Investigation. I wonder if I could have a minute of your time."

The woman next to her bristled. She was older and rounder than Megan Vance but shared the same brilliant green eyes. The sister, he guessed. "She's told you all what happened a million times already. How many times do you people have to put her through this?"

"Molly, it's all right," Megan said, her voice quiet but determined. "Will you grab another cup of coffee for me? Agent Davis?"

He shook his head. The sister looked reluctant, but she rose and left them alone.

Megan Vance faced him, her hands tight together and her remarkable eyes filled with raw emotion. For one insane moment, he was stunned and appalled by his urge to gather her close and promise everything would be all right. He shoved it away.

"I'm very sorry about your son, but I can assure you many excellent people will be helping in the search."

She drew in a slow breath and when she met his gaze, he could see a layer of steel underneath the pain.

"I don't need platitudes, Agent Davis. I need action. Why is everyone standing around and not out there looking for my son?"

He had to respect her grit. "It's very important in cases like this not to go racing off in a hundred different directions and run the risk of trampling over your son's trail. When the sun comes up in an hour or so, you'll see everybody here jump into action."

"I can't stand that he's out there in the dark somewhere. I need to be out looking for him."

Despite his best efforts to remain impartial, the emotion in her voice seemed to slither through his defenses.

"I know it's tough but the best thing you can do for Cameron right now is to help us narrow the direction of our search. Would you mind going over the timeline with me?"

After a moment, she nodded. "I put him to bed as usual at about 9:00 p.m. He was sleeping soundly at ten when I checked on him—I tucked the blanket up so I know for sure he was in bed at that time. I woke at two and went to check on him and he was gone."

"What woke you?"

She paused slightly. "I had a nightmare."

"Is that unusual for you?"

"Not really."

"And do you usually check your children when you wake from a bad dream in the middle of the night?"

He hadn't meant to make his questions sound like an interrogation, but her mouth tightened.

"Look, Agent Davis, I know the drill here. I've watched enough television to know you have to consider me a suspect. I have no problem with that. None whatsoever. Take my DNA, my fingerprints, whatever. I'll take a lie detector test or anything else you want. But please hurry, so you can quickly rule me out and focus on finding my son."

Chapter 2

6:32 a.m.

He was in serious trouble.

Cameron hit the glow on his watch and groaned at the time. His mom was going to have a total cow. Most mornings she got up early to work in her office before he and Hailey woke up. If she checked on him like she usually did, by now she had probably found the stupid wadded blankets he thought had been such a great idea.

It seemed like such a baby thing to do now, something even Hailey could come up with.

If she had checked on him like usual, she must have figured out he was gone. He felt sick to his stomach just thinking about how worried she must be. She totally freaked out if he even walked an aisle away from her at the grocery store.

Had she called the police? Gosh, he hoped so. He thought of that terrible scream and the thud of a body falling and shivered in the cool, damp air, wishing he had the new jacket he'd taken off inside the entrance.

He had been lost in the maze of tunnels for more than four hours, and he had to admit that he was starting to get a little nervous about finding his way out again.

Like an idiot, he had gone way too far into the mine after that gunshot. He had just wanted to escape that ugly scene. By now, he was so turned around he didn't know which way he'd come.

None of this seemed familiar. These tunnels were more narrow, barely wide enough for him to get through in spots.

He had tried to backtrack but was now more confused than ever.

His night vision goggles were worthless in here with no light to draw on, so he had abandoned them a ways back and pulled his flashlight out of his bag.

He wasn't completely unprepared. He might have made mistakes, but at least he hadn't been *that* stupid. After he first found the mine entrance a few weeks earlier, he had checked out a book on spelunking from the library, slipping it between a book on soccer and a middle reader mystery so his mom wouldn't see it and suspect anything.

The book said to always wear a helmet for head protection when exploring underground places. A caver could bump his head on a low ceiling if he wasn't careful.

All he had was his bike helmet so he had used that. He was grateful for it now since he'd already bonked his head twice in the low tunnels.

The book also said to take along three sources of illumination. Besides the now-worthless night vision goggles, he had two flashlights with two extra sets of batteries for each.

They weren't going to last long, he knew. Since he was taking a short break, he turned off the flashlight for now to conserve energy, grateful it hung on a lanyard around his neck so he couldn't lose it. That was a trick his dad taught him when they used to go fishing and stuff, always to keep his light handy.

His dad would have been really mad at him for worrying his mom like this.

He sighed, taking a sip from one of two water bottles he'd stowed in his backpack earlier that evening. He also had a couple of granola bars, some hard candy and a banana.

Without his mom seeing, he had also managed to sneak a few other survival items out of his dad's stuff stored in the garage, like a first aid kit, one of those shiny survival blankets and a lighter.

He didn't dare use the lighter inside the mine, though. He knew enough from reading that spelunking book to know there could be bad air inside these places and he didn't want to risk it.

He looked at his watch again: six forty-five. How long would it take the police to start looking for him? And how would they ever figure out he was inside here, trapped in miles of tunnels with a dead guy?

He shivered again, wishing with all his heart he was

back in his bed complaining at his mom for coming in to wake him up so soon.

8:15 a.m.

The community had turned out in force.

Megan stood on her porch and looked out at the crowds of volunteer searchers waiting for assignments to begin combing the foothills above her house.

The sun had barely crested the mountains to the east, but already an empty field at the edge of her five acres had been turned into a staging area for the search.

A Moose Springs Search and Rescue trailer served as the mobile command center, and she could see horses and all-terrain vehicles being unloaded and dozens of strangers with water bottles and fanny packs milling around as the various agencies involved worked out all the necessary search details.

How could this all have happened so suddenly? The FBI agent had been right. Once the sun rose, the search effort had ramped up significantly. Now everything looked organized and efficient. For the first time since she found that horribly empty bed, hope began to flutter through her.

"Looks like word travels fast."

She turned to find the FBI agent who had grilled her for more than an hour. Caleb Davis stood on the edge of the porch. She didn't know if he watched her or the volunteer searchers, since dark sunglasses shielded his eyes.

Megan had to fight down her instinctive defensiveness, her deep sense of invasion at the questions he had asked. She knew he had only been doing his job, and she knew later she would probably appreciate his thoroughness. But the hour spent under his microscope had been grueling and intrusive.

Can you go over what woke you again? What led you to go into Cameron's room? Do you often check on him in the night?

He had asked the questions a dozen different ways. His voice had been cool, controlled, but all the time he questioned her, Agent Davis had studied her out of polar-blue eyes that looked as if they could pierce titanium.

She had answered his questions over and over, never wavering in her story. She still couldn't tell whether or not he believed her story from any reaction on his lean, harshly handsome features. At this point, she didn't give a damn. She just wanted her son home—and she could only pray the people gathering in that meadow down there could facilitate that.

"They don't even know us," she spoke her thoughts aloud. "Where are they all coming from?"

Agent Davis removed his sunglasses. Their gazes met and for an instant she almost thought she saw a slight softening of his hard edges. It disappeared so quickly she wondered if she had imagined it.

"A missing child usually rallies the troops," he answered. "I should warn you that all indicators are predicting this will be one of those high-profile, media circus kind of cases, especially given your late husband's military record and the urgency of Cameron's medical condition."

The very idea turned her stomach. She had faced enough cameras after Rick's death to last a lifetime. The San Diego media had jumped on the story of a home-town hero dying in a secret rescue mission in Afghanistan. News vans had been parked on her street for a good two weeks after his funeral, and she and the children had been virtually cloistered inside her house.

Though she had tried to be a good example of a strong, resilient military wife, the newspaper photographs had plainly showed the ravaging grief she hadn't been able to hide.

"Don't be surprised when more searchers and more media representatives show up as the day goes on," Agent Davis continued. "Unfortunately, people around here have had probably too much experience with this sort of thing. Seems like every summer a Boy Scout gets separated from his troop and disappears in the Uintas."

"Are they all eventually found?"

A muscle flexed in his jaw but he didn't answer her. She was suddenly chilled from more than just the cool morning air. She gripped the railing so hard the wood dug into her flesh. "I want to search. I need to do something."

Again, she thought she saw a flicker of compassion in his eyes, quickly veiled.

Why was he so hesitant to show any emotion? she wondered, then pushed the thought away. She didn't care. He could be made up of nothing but granite as long as he helped find her son.

"It would be best if you stayed close to the house in case we have more questions for you."

"Would you stay put if your child were out there somewhere?"

She didn't wait for an answer, just hurried down the porch steps toward the bustling activity, driven only by this raging need inside her to act.

As she hurried across her property, she was aware of Caleb Davis dogging her steps. Was he suddenly her designated handler? she wondered. She wanted nothing more than to escape those piercing blue eyes, but she had a feeling he wasn't an easy man to evade.

At least she had managed to lose Molly for now. Her sister had returned to her house down the road to check on Hailey and make sure she was comfortably settled with Molly's four kids and her husband, Scott. They would shower her daughter with attention, Megan knew, and keep Hailey busy and distracted so she wouldn't spend all her time worrying about the brother she adored.

She only wished she could be so lucky, but she knew nothing would distract her from this grinding fear inside her.

With no real plan in mind, only this urgency to act, she hurried up the metal steps to the command trailer. As soon as she opened the door, she realized this had been a mistake.

A group of men and women filled every available space inside the trailer and they were all listening to Sheriff Galvez give instructions. He broke off when he caught sight of her, his dark eyes suddenly filling with a compassion she saw mirrored on the faces of everyone else inside the trailer.

She shouldn't have interrupted them. All she had done was distract them from the search effort.

Painfully aware of Agent Davis behind her, no doubt watching her out of those sharp, piercing eyes, she cleared her throat. "Hello. I'm sorry. I…I didn't mean to interrupt. I just wanted to tell you all thank-you for what you're doing. Please find my son."

"We'll do the best we can." A round, balding man she thought she had met at church spoke up.

...ang in there, Megan," said Wayne Shumway, ...her clients at her CPA firm. She had a vague ...ry of him asking her if the Internal Revenue Service would let him write off his training expenses for the time he contributed to the county's volunteer search and rescue team.

Their sympathy was suddenly more than she could bear. She wouldn't have believed it, but she almost thought she preferred the FBI agent's cool impassivity to this cloying, smothering compassion.

She mustered a smile, murmured another thank-you, then hurried from the command center.

Her emotions were thick and close to the surface as she hurried out of the trailer, so heavy inside her she staggered under the weight of them. An overwhelming, helpless fear was foremost among them, and she had to stop a few dozen yards from the trailer and close her eyes, whispering another hurried prayer for her son's safe return.

When she opened her eyes, she found the FBI agent beside her, watching her with that same carefully neutral expression. She wanted to lash out at something and Caleb Davis happened to be the most convenient target just now.

"Don't you have anything better to do than follow me around?" she snapped. "I don't need a watchdog."

He raised a dark, slashing eyebrow. "How about a friend?"

"You're not my friend. We both know that." To her horror, her voice trembled on the last word and suddenly her anger disappeared as quickly as it had erupted. All her emotions bubbled closer to the surface, threatening to spill over.

She blinked them back fiercely, aware of the FBI agent studying her. After a moment, he made a sighing kind of sound and pulled a handkerchief out of his pocket, an old-fashioned white one like her father used to carry. It took her by surprise and also sent a few of those tears leaking out.

She sniffled for a moment into his handkerchief but regained control quickly. She couldn't afford to break down, not when Cameron needed her. She lifted her face to the warm summer sun, wondering how such a horrible thing could happen on a day that looked so beautiful.

The heavy rains of the night before left the morning fresh and clean and gorgeous, the kind of day she had come to love in the few months she had been in Utah.

A light wind poured off the mountains, sweet with pine and sage from the acres of national forest land bordering her property. After growing up in Boston and spending all her married life in the hustle of San Diego, she found she loved living out here on the edge of the wilderness, watching mule deer forage in her garden, listening to the shrill cry of hawks overhead and the distant yip of coyotes in the evening.

Now she hated it. Cameron could be anywhere out in that vast tract of land—and that was the best-case scenario. She couldn't bear thinking that someone might have broken into her house and taken him under her very nose.

She drew a shuddering breath, feeling again the watchful gaze of Caleb Davis. She knew she was at the top of the suspect list right now, as far as the FBI agent was concerned. The knowledge burned, but she knew she couldn't let it get to her.

"Tell me, Agent Davis. How many missing child cases have you investigated?"

If she hadn't been looking closely at him, she might have missed the slight twitch of a muscle in his jaw before his expression returned to impassivity.

"A few," he answered.

Some demon compelled her to push him. "Too many to count?"

"Seventy-nine, in the eight years I've been with the FBI's Crimes Against Children unit."

Seventy-nine. She shivered at the number, at the pain she knew it must represent, and at his preciseness in remembering it. All that heartache. She couldn't bear it.

"How many of those have been resolved in a way you would deem successful?"

She didn't want to ask but couldn't seem to help herself. *Not enough.*

He didn't say the words, but she could see them in the sudden flare of darkness in the clear depths of his eyes. The unsaid message hovered between them, dank and ugly, and then he veiled his expression again.

"I know it's an impossible thing to ask, Mrs. Vance, but you can't think about those other children. All your energy right now should be focused on your own son."

Before she could answer, the door of the command center trailer opened and the rescuers emerged into the sunlight. Daniel Galvez was the last to leave. He caught sight of them standing near the fence and walked to them. Megan was aware of the careful way he looked at her, as if he were afraid she would break apart right in front of him.

She felt like it, but she managed to hold on to whatever remnants of control she had left.

She was more surprised when he gave the same concerned scrutiny to Caleb Davis.

"Don't even ask. I'm fine," the FBI agent growled.

She gazed between the two men, baffled at their byplay. "I'm sure you are," the sheriff said. "McKinnon wouldn't have brought you back for this one if you weren't."

Davis said nothing. He just put his sunglasses back on.

Megan finally broke the awkward silence. "I'm sorry I interrupted you back there," she said again.

The sheriff turned his attention to her. "Don't worry about it. You should be included in the loop—I promise I'll do my best to keep you informed of the search logistics. The first wave of searchers is already out there combing the grid, and another wave is receiving instructions so they can leave shortly. Search dogs will be here in the next hour or so, though the rain of last night and the wind that's predicted to pick up in a couple hours may hamper their efforts."

She was aware of Caleb Davis standing beside her, ever watchful. She found a strange comfort in his presence, though it made absolutely no sense, given his hour-long interrogation of her.

"Thank you," she said to Daniel. "I do appreciate knowing what's happening. Please, Sheriff, what can I do?"

He sighed and gestured to the news vans jockeying for position down the road. "I hate to burden you with this right now, but the media is already clamoring for some kind of statement from the family. You don't have to say anything if you don't want to. But we do need to get the word out that Cameron's missing, in case some-one might have seen something. Do you feel up to talk-ing to the press?"

She pressed a hand to her stomach at the instinctive recoil there. How could she possibly stand before the harsh glare of cameras and strip her soul bare? Could she endure that sense of invasion again, that emotional purge? Her nails dug into her palms. She would hate it. But for Cameron she would endure anything.

"Mrs. Vance, may I make a suggestion?"

She turned to Agent Davis. "Of course."

"Quite often in cases like this, the immediate family of a missing child appoints a spokesperson to handle the media, to make public statements, address media re-quests, that sort of thing. Perhaps your sister or brother-in-law would be willing to take care of that burden for you until you feel up to the challenge of facing the media."

She seized on the idea. "I'll talk to Molly when she returns from checking on Hailey."

"I believe I saw her Expedition pull up a few min-utes ago." Daniel gestured to the row of vehicles in the driveway.

She followed his gaze and saw with mixed emo-tions that her sister had indeed returned. She must be inside the house.

As much as she needed Molly right now, she dreaded seeing her own fear reflected in her sister's eyes.

"Thank you. I'll go talk to her now," she said.

She walked away from the two men, painfully aware of them watching her every step of the way.

Did the sheriff suspect her of harming her son, as well? She had met him a few times in town, and he had always been friendly and approachable. She hated that he might suspect her of something terrible.

Oh, she couldn't bear this. She just wanted Cameron in her arms again and for all these people to be gone so she and her family could get back to the business of life.

Cale watched Megan Vance climb the redwood steps of the back deck leading to her house. She paused for a moment on the steps, her head angled toward a lone soccer ball rolled into a corner of the deck. Even from here he could see her shoulders slump, fear and tension in every line of her slender form.

She looked more breakable with each passing moment. He could only hope she had a good support system, that her sister could help pull her through.

She was going to need all the help she could get.

He hated this part of his job, dealing with the tumult of emotions in those left behind.

An image of Amanda Decker's wild rage two weeks earlier lashed him. *Why couldn't you save them?* she had half sobbed, half screamed. *You were right there! Why couldn't you help them?*

He knew she had only been speaking out of grief and shock, but her words had been like hydrochloric acid on his already raw emotions. Later she had visited him in the hospital to apologize for her outburst and to thank him for his efforts, but it didn't take away the searing guilt.

Cale mentally kicked himself. He couldn't afford to think about Mirabel and Soshi Decker right now. He hadn't been able to help them, but his complete and abject failure in that case didn't mean he couldn't help Cameron Vance and his pale, fragile mother.

"What's your gut telling you on this one?" Daniel Galvez asked him. "In my book, Megan Vance is either one hell of an actress or she had nothing whatsoever to do with her son's disappearance. You think we're looking at some kind of stranger abduction?"

He jerked his mind away from the image of two little coffins being lowered into the ground and made himself focus on this case. "We've got to consider every option here. The window was open. Even though it's a second story, someone determined enough could find a way to get in and take the boy."

"But why bother to stage things with the old pillow-under-the-blankets gag to fake out the mother?" Galvez asked. "That's the kind of thing a kid would do on his own, don't you think?"

He pondered the details he had learned from his interview with Megan Vance. "If someone knew the mother was a light sleeper and that she made it a habit to check on the children in the night—especially the boy with his medical condition—they might have been trying to buy a little more time."

"How would a stranger know that?"

"Damn good question." One he unfortunately couldn't answer at this point in the investigation. "Where do things stand with the state crime scene unit?"

"They're still working the boy's room. Mrs. Vance just cleaned the room two days ago. Because the kid has allergies, too, she's a pretty thorough housekeeper in there. Preliminary reports showed no sign of forced entry and no fingerprints but family members'. Megan's and Cameron's are the only ones we can find on the window or the windowsill. I think CSU is still working the scene if you want to hear the details from them."

"I'll do that. Thanks."

At that moment, someone came out of the command center and called for the sheriff's attention. Galvez sighed and turned away. "Let me know if you need any other information," he said to Cale before he headed back the way he had come.

Cale paused for a moment, looking at the bustle of activity. Then on impulse, he walked around the house to check the perimeter of the building for more clues. He was pleased to find a state crime scene detective he had worked with before, Wilhelmina Carson, taking pictures of the outside of the two-story log home.

"Hey, Willy. What have you got out here?"

"Hang on," she ordered in a distracted voice, still clicking away. After a few more shots, she dropped the camera and he saw surprise register in her eyes when she recognized him.

"Davis! I hadn't heard you were back on the job."

How long would it take before people stopped looking at him as if he were going to go freaking mental at any minute?

"You know me. I can't stay away."

She cleared her throat and he braced himself for what he knew was coming. "I'm really sorry about what happened to you, Cale," she said quietly. "I worked the Decker scene. I know you did everything you could."

He wasn't sure he would ever be as convinced about that as everyone else seemed to be, but this wasn't the place to argue the point. Instead, he gestured to the home's exterior. "Have you seen any sign at all of forced entry?"

After a moment, she turned back to the case, though he could still see concern in her eyes. "Not much. The screen was in backward, with the tabs on the outside, indicating whoever put it back did it from out here. I don't know if that's significant at all."

"No ladder impressions or anything like that?"

"Nothing. But keep in mind we had a solid rain for two hours between 3:00 and 5:00 a.m. That's a sure way to screw up a crime scene."

Which meant someone could have used a ladder or driven up to the house with a damn cherry picker, for all the evidence they could find.

He studied the exterior of the building. It was a straight shot from the boy's second story window to the ground. He supposed it was possible Cameron could have jumped, but that was a mighty long way down for a nine-year-old kid.

When he was nine, he used to escape the hell of home by climbing out a conveniently situated tree out his bedroom window whenever he could. The only tree near Cameron Vance's bedroom was a sycamore a dozen feet from the house. Though the trunk was thick and sturdy, no branches extended anywhere near the kid's room.

He studied the distance. No way. The tree was too far from the house to provide any kind of useful escape route.

So how would he climb out the window to the ground if he were trying to sneak out in the night? If his shoulder didn't have a bullet hole in it, he probably would extend out the window, grab hold of the roof line and move hand over hand to the corner of the house, where he could use the gutter spout to climb down, praying the whole way down it would hold his weight.

But he had two feet in height over the kid and years of climbing experience.

He looked at the log exterior of the house again and this time caught sight of something he'd missed before.

"Son of a bitch," he exclaimed, moving closer for a better look.

he opened and squeezed softly toward of his nape,
where he reached up the pause against to clear. Your
pray in the so dump drew it turned to the strange
Any, it had been left to a job that ever you too were
summoning our coher all.

He looked at the expression in the mirror again and
this time though suppled something, he rubbed before.
Second it upon these intend awoing abose that
where their feeling of this old.

Chapter 3

"What have you got?" Willy hurried toward him, her
gaze sharp and intent.

He was always glad to work a case with the detective. She had a quick, analytical mind and always took
a second or third look at the facts to make sure she
wasn't missing anything.

She wasn't bad on the eyes, either, with tawny skin
and the long-legged grace of a natural athlete. Not that
he had ever spent much time noticing, but maybe he
should. These last few weeks had made him painfully
aware of the loneliness of his life outside of work.
Somehow he had focused all his energy on the job,
leaving nothing for a personal life.

When the job went wrong, he had been left with
nothing.

Not that he wanted that kind of complication right

now. But if he did, he ought to think about hooking up with someone tough-shelled and resilient, like Wilhelmina Carson.

He certainly wouldn't be stupid enough to waste his time taking a second look at someone breakable like Megan Vance.

"Did I miss something?" Willy asked.

He put any thought of soft, fragile women out of his head, then slipped off his shoes and socks, gauging the wall carefully as he did. "I don't know. See those holes up there?"

She looked baffled but studied where he pointed. "Those little things? I thought they were just screwholes or imperfections in the logs or something."

"They're a little too evenly spaced to be imperfections. Hang on."

He stuck the index finger of his right hand in the lowest three-quarter-inch hole, then extended his left hand to the next highest. Pain radiated from his shoulder but he ignored it, as he'd been trying to do for two long weeks. As he suspected, the holes were about three feet apart, just about the width of a nine-year-old's outstretched fingers.

"Damn. This kid is amazing."

Ignoring the strident cry of protest from his shoulder, he pulled himself up the logs using the conveniently placed fingerholes, pausing about halfway between the ground and the boy's window.

"You are frigging crazy, Davis!"

Below, he caught a clear view of Willy's consternation. "You're two weeks out of having your shoulder ripped open, you idiot. Let me find you a damn ladder."

"I'm good. Just hang on."

"Do I have to go find McKinnon to drag you down?"

Okay, this hadn't been the smartest idea. His shoulder wasn't anywhere near ready for this, especially when he was wearing a shirt and tie and his second-best summer weight slacks instead of Lycra and climbing shoes.

"I'm done." He jumped the five feet to the ground. "You're going to want to find that ladder now and dust those finger holes I didn't use for prints."

"You really think the boy climbed out on his own using those dinky finger holes?"

"Wouldn't be the first time a kid climbed out an open window."

"That took time and effort to drill those holes. This wasn't something that happened overnight. Could someone else be involved?"

"Possibly, but I'm beginning to doubt it. Those holes are custom-set for a nine-year-old's arm span. Did you notice how awkward they were for me to use, spaced so close together?"

Willy shook her head in disbelief. "All I saw was an agent with the Federal Bureau of Idiots trying to kill himself. Good grief, Davis. This kid is only nine years old! How the hell could he pull it off?"

"My guess is practice. The holes are already worn in spots."

"That would explain why the boy's fingerprints are the only ones I can find on the window ledge. Am I wasting my time looking for evidence somebody else was involved in the kid's disappearance, then?"

His gut was telling him the boy escaped completely on his own, for reasons Cale didn't yet understand.

He really hoped that was the case, for the mother's sake, and that searchers would find him camped out in the mountains somewhere oblivious to all the trouble he had left behind.

"It's never a waste of time to check out all the angles. I could be completely off base here."

"But you don't think so."

"You didn't hear it from me," he answered. "Until we know otherwise with absolute certainty, the FBI will continue working this case as a possible abduction."

And he would do his best not to spend more time than absolutely necessary dwelling on the missing boy's mother, with her soft skin and her scared eyes.

12:25 p.m.

This wasn't the right way, either.

In the fading light of his flashlight, Cameron saw a huge pile of rubble blocking the shaft he had been certain would take him back to familiar ground.

He turned off the flashlight to conserve whatever juice he had left and slumped to the ground, feeling worse than the time his soccer team back in San Diego had lost the championship game in the league playoffs by one stinking last-minute goal.

He pressed one hand to his whirly stomach and used the other to wipe away the hot tears burning his eyes. He had been so sure this way would lead him back to the tunnels he had explored, where he could follow his own chalk marks back to the entrance and go home.

Home.

He wanted so much to be there, safe in his own room

with the pictures of his dad on the wall and his soccer trophies on a shelf by his bed.

He sniffled, wiping his nose on his shirt. Was anybody looking for him yet? He could bet his uncle and cousins were out there. But his stomach hurt even worse thinking about it. Nobody would have any idea where to look for him, and that was the scariest thing of all.

He knew a good Navy SEAL left no trace behind him, and Cam had been careful to wipe away his tracks leading into the shaft and to cover the entrance with a dead sagebrush.

If only he hadn't been so careful, maybe someone would find the mine entrance and figure out he was in here.

He never knew dark could be so *dark*. It was heavy and scary—he couldn't even see his own hand when he held it right up to his eyes.

The two times he had sneaked into the tunnels before, he hadn't stayed very long and he had always had plenty of light. It had been more exciting than scary, like exploring a whole new planet somewhere that nobody else knew about.

It was exciting then. Now the dark was so heavy and sometimes he couldn't even tell whether his eyes were open or closed.

He had two more sets of batteries and a spare flashlight, but he didn't know how long he was going to be in here. He didn't want to use all his light and then be left with nothing.

He didn't want to die in the dark somewhere, alone and scared. He wiped his nose again, wondering what he should do. He had turned so many corners in the mine that he didn't have the first idea which way would lead him out.

Overwhelmed by his fear and at the thought of dying, he couldn't keep in a sob. He cried for a minute, then tried to stop. He wasn't making any progress sitting here like a big baby and bawling his eyes out. Every minute he wasted was another minute he had to stay in the dark.

His breath came in little baby gasps, but he managed to quit bawling after another minute or two. He would say a prayer, he decided. That's what his mom told him to do whenever he was worried or scared or hurting.

Though he whispered the words, they sounded loud and echoing in the total quiet of the tunnel.

"Help me out of here, please. I promise if You do, I'll never sneak out at night again, even when I'm a teenager, and I won't yell at my sister when she touches my stuff. I'll share my PlayStation with her and I won't talk back to my mom, even in my head."

He paused, not sure what else to say. "You know," he said after a minute, "I could really use my dad's help in here. If he's not busy, could You send him down to help me out? Amen."

He felt a little better after he prayed, though he had to admit to some disappointment when the way out of the mine shaft didn't suddenly glow in front of him in big flashing lights.

After a minute, when nothing supermiraculous happened, such as his dad's angel suddenly showing up, he sighed and pulled the water bottle out of his pack, allowing himself just a tiny sip.

He was so thirsty he wanted to suck down the whole thing, but he knew that would be a bad idea. He might need some later.

He would just go back the way he had come this time

and try a different route. Sooner or later, he would find his way out.

He stood up, then remembered something else and raised his eyes to the ceiling of the chamber. "One more thing," he prayed out loud. "Can You please help my mom not to be so mad at me?"

1:30 p.m.

She was suffocating under the weight of all the solicitude being piled on her.

Just now it was her big sister adding another layer.

"Honey, you can't stay here all day," Molly entreated, her green eyes dark and worried. "Why don't you come on back to our place where things are a little more quiet and rest for a while?"

"I can't leave right now," she said firmly.

"Our house is just down the road. You know Daniel will let us know the minute they find him."

She deeply appreciated her sister's stubborn optimism, but she still wasn't willing to leave the house. Not until Cam was found.

"You go, Mol," she replied. "I know you're exhausted from that press conference."

Megan couldn't help thinking Molly was the one who looked as if she needed to rest. Her pretty soccer mom of a sister looked ravaged, totally wiped out by the stress of this ordeal.

Guilt pinched at her. Had she asked too much of Molly to put her in front of the cameras?

"I'm fine," Molly answered. "I only hope whatever I said to the media will somehow help us find Cam."

"It will."

She hugged her sister, thinking how much she owed her. Molly had been there any time Megan needed her, a quiet, steady source of strength and support.

Megan had been twelve, Molly nineteen—a freshman in college—when the cancer that had ravaged their mother for more than a year ultimately took Carol Kincaid's life. Megan could never forget that her sister had left school and returned home to Boston to care for her and Kevin, their brother who had been fourteen at the time.

When other girls her age were busy with boyfriends and algebra finals and trips to Cancun for spring break, Molly had been home with them doing laundry, fixing lunches, helping with homework. She never complained, but Megan knew it couldn't have been easy on her.

A year later, they were all barely beginning to find their way through the grief over their mother's death when the unthinkable happened—their police officer father was struck and killed by a drunk driver while he was standing on the side of the road giving a routine traffic ticket.

With patience and love, Molly had pulled her and Kevin through the devastating pain. Completely on her own, her twenty-year-old sister had kept their little family together for three years until Kevin left for college.

By then she'd started dating a handsome young law student. Megan didn't think her sister ever would have married the love of her life until Megan reached adulthood if she hadn't interfered.

One night when Molly had been busy in the kitchen, she had taken Scott Randall aside and told him bluntly that if he wanted to marry her sister, Megan would be happy to go live with friends for the remaining two years of high school so they wouldn't have to start married life with an annoying teenage girl underfoot.

Scott had been surprised at first at her bluntness, then had laughed, hugged her, then pulled out of his pocket the ring he planned to give to Molly that very night.

Together, the two of them had worked for two weeks to convince Molly there was no obstacle to her marrying the man of her dreams.

They had all grieved together on 9/11 when their New York firefighter brother had died running into Tower One of the World Trade Center. And Scott and Molly had packed up their family and come to stay for a month in San Diego after Rick's death.

She knew she relied on her sister's strength too much. At some point she needed to stand on her own.

But not now. She couldn't survive this without her sister's help—and she knew Megan would use up every bit of her emotional reserves if she didn't convince her to rest.

"Go on home and take it easy. Scott and the kids need you and so does Hailey. I'll let you know how things are going here."

Molly looked torn. "Are you sure?"

She nodded firmly. "Go."

"All right. I'll take a few hours to check on things at home and make sure nobody's set the house on fire. You take care of yourself while I'm gone, promise? You need to rest and eat something, honey."

"I will," she lied.

Her sister kissed her cheek, and the worry in her eyes took Megan's breath away. Somehow, seeing the edge of panic in her sister who was usually so calm and in control seemed to magnify Megan's own gut-wrenching fear.

After her sister left, she crossed to the window above the sink and looked out at the mountains behind her house. As the weather forecasters had warned, a hot, dry wind blew down the mountains, rattling the branches of the crabapple tree outside her kitchen window and fluttering the heads of the daisies and columbines in her flower garden.

People were coming and going in every direction. Megan had never felt so helpless.

This was the first time she had been completely alone since she had called the police and then Molly in the early hours of the morning. It had been hard enough keeping her fear under control in the presence of others. She found it impossible when only in the company of her own terrible thoughts.

Where could he be? Was he safe? Why hadn't they found him yet?

She knew there were several theories buzzing around the command center. There were no doubt some—like Agent Davis—who suspected she had harmed Cam in some way and then had reported him missing to cover up her heinous crime.

Though it stung to know people might be so cynical, she couldn't really blame them. She supposed it was logical to look at those closest to the child in cases like this. Knowing that, though, didn't make the shame of those suspicions any easier to bear.

She knew there were also those who believed Cam might have wandered away. If that was the case, why hadn't they found him yet? The mountains were vast, but he was just a nine-year-old boy. He couldn't have wandered *that* far.

Still, that was far easier to digest than the third alternative, that someone had taken him out of his bedroom for reasons she couldn't even bear thinking about.

She had no enemies in Moose Springs, no one willing to exact revenge on her through her child. She knew only a few people—some clients, some of her sister's friends, a handful of people she'd met at church. If this had been a random act, why target Cameron?

Please keep him safe, she prayed silently as a thousand doubts and fears stampeded over her.

"Mrs. Vance? Are you okay?"

She opened her eyes and saw with some degree of consternation that the grim-faced FBI agent had entered the kitchen. He had changed from his suit to jeans and a black T-shirt with FBI on the back and he studied her with an odd look in those icy blue eyes—a strange mix of concern and reluctance, as if he hadn't expected to find her here.

"No. I'm sorry, but I'm not okay." She didn't know if she ever would be again.

"Did your sister leave?"

"I sent her home to get some rest," she answered. "The press conference exhausted her."

"Did you watch any of it?"

She nodded. "As much as I could stand. I had to turn it off near the end."

She had had enough after the media started asking questions about Rick's death and the stress a grieving widow must be facing as she raised two young children on her own.

"Your sister was a perfect spokesperson—calm and controlled, but impassioned and forceful at the same time."

"That's Molly in a nutshell."

He looked as if he wanted to say something else and continued to study her with that probing look she found so uncomfortable.

"Was there something you needed, Agent Davis?" she asked when the silence between them stretched on a little too awkwardly. She deliberately used his title and that seemed to jar him back to awareness.

He blinked. "Right. I came in for a drink. That hot wind out there is a killer."

Between the rain of the night before and the hot dry wind today, conditions couldn't have been more unfavorable for tracking one missing little boy.

"I hope the searchers are keeping hydrated."

"They're all under strict orders, eight ounces of water for every hour they're out in the sun." He paused. "You know they had to call off the search dogs, don't you?"

She nodded tightly. She had been devastated when Daniel Galvez had told her the news, explaining that the swirling wind and the volunteer searchers were all muddying the scent and the dogs hadn't been able to pick anything up.

"The handlers will take them out again tonight after they've rested, when it's cooler and the wind dies down," Agent Davis said. "They might have better luck then."

Nighttime. She couldn't bear to think of Cam being out there somewhere in the dark, alone and wanting his mother. Even more frightening, each tick of the clock was one more minute he spent without his life-saving seizure medication.

"Do you know anything about epilepsy, Agent Davis?"

He finished a swallow of his water before answering. "Some. My first partner had a sister with it."

"My son suffers from grand mal seizures. After much trial and error, we've been lucky to find a medicine combination that has worked for him for the last few years. As long as he takes his meds twice a day, his seizures are controlled. He's now missed one dose. By this evening he'll have missed two doses. He's out there somewhere, and every moment that passes until we find him puts him in more jeopardy of having a seizure that could kill him."

Chapter 4

She had nothing to do with her son's disappearance.

Cale wasn't sure exactly what convinced him in her impassioned speech. He only knew that as he listened to her, he realized he could never believe she was hiding anything about her son or her treatment of him.

Megan Vance was exactly as she seemed—a frightened mother worried for her child. He would bet his reputation on it.

He had put his trust in the wrong people a few times before. He didn't know anybody in the Bureau who hadn't made some mistakes. But something told him, without any shadow of doubt, that this wouldn't be one of those times.

He believed her. Though he had tried to keep an open mind and consider the possibility that she might have harmed her son and filed a false missing persons report, he just couldn't buy it. Nothing in her background or in her behavior set off any red flags.

Not only did he want to trust her, he wanted to help her find whatever measure of peace might be possible under the circumstances.

"I'm sorry, Mrs. Vance," he said quietly. "I know this is terrible for you. But there are hundreds of people out there doing everything possible to find your son before that happens."

She nodded tightly and let out a shaky breath. "I know that. This waiting is just so horrible."

He had seen it in every one of those seventy-nine missing child cases he had worked. Sometimes parents only had to wait and hour or two. Others waited days, holding out a frantic hope only to see it cruelly dashed when their child's body was found.

He thought of Lynn and Sam McKinnon, the parents of his partner Gage. Their daughter Charlotte had been stolen from them at age three from their Las Vegas front yard. For nearly twenty-four years, they had never given up hope of finding her, though the girl's disappearance had haunted the family every day for decades.

And then, when they should have lost all hope, Charlotte had been miraculously returned to them.

The McKinnons had lost their daughter's childhood, but they had her back with them again. He knew plenty of parents who still waited and would probably never find the answers they sought.

He could only hope Megan Vance wouldn't be one of them.

"You shouldn't be waiting alone. Isn't there someone who could sit with you?"

Someone besides me, he thought. An FBI agent who had spent years slogging through the absolute worst humanity dished out against the innocent was probably not the most comforting companion for a parent in crisis looking for hope and encouragement.

Her lovely features twisted into a grimace. "I sent everyone away. I swear, if one more person pats my hand and asks me how I'm holding up, I'm going to rip somebody's eyeballs out."

He blinked rapidly, surprised to find himself smiling a little. After the last two weeks, he hadn't been sure he would be able to find anything to smile about again. How strange that he should find it in the frustrated words of a terrified mother.

He leaned a hip against the counter. "Do me a favor and keep your hands in your pockets, then, just in case I happen to forget that I've been duly warned."

Though she didn't smile in return, the tightness of her features eased a little.

They lapsed into silence and he sipped his water, wishing he had some comfort to offer. His mind pored over the facts of the case, his working theory right now that the boy had climbed out on his own.

She might be able to shed some light on a few inconsistencies in the case.

"Mrs. Vance—"

"Megan, please," she said.

"Megan." It was a lovely name, one that, combined with her green eyes and vibrant hair, made him think of fairy sprites and rolling fields of clover and…

He broke off the thought. Where the hell had that

come from? He was here to do a job, not suddenly wax poetic over a woman's name.

Annoyed at himself, his voice came out more brusque than he intended. "I know Cameron had epilepsy. Do you think that hinders his physical abilities at all?"

Her brow furrowed. "I'm not sure what you mean."

"How athletic is your son?"

She sighed. "More than I have ever been comfortable with, if you want to know the truth. Because of his condition, I've always been a little overprotective, afraid he'll have a seizure in the middle of doing something physical and hurt himself. It's easy to forget that beyond his epilepsy, he's just a typical boy who loves sports. Everything physical—soccer, basketball, baseball. You name it."

"I noticed your son has some pictures in his room of your late husband in climbing gear."

She smiled, though it didn't quite reach her eyes. "I guess you could say Rick was an adrenaline junkie. He always skied black diamond runs, kayaked Class Five rapids and climbed any route above a 5.8."

There were some who would put Cale in that same category. When he wasn't working, he was usually heading to southern Utah to bike the slickrock or go canyoneering through the slots. Adrenaline junkie was probably an accurate term.

"What about you?" he asked Megan.

A corner of her mouth lifted, though the worry in her eyes robbed the expression of any semblance to a smile. Seeing her halfhearted effort still gave him a catch in his chest and he was astonished to find himself wondering what a full-on smile from her would look like.

"I knit, Agent Davis. That's about as exciting as I get."

"You never joined your husband when he climbed?"

She shrugged. "I went along a few times when Rick and I were first dating. Trying to be a good girlfriend, you know, interested in the things he liked to do. But I'm not crazy about heights, and he figured that out pretty quickly and wouldn't let me harness up anymore. After that, I just took along a book, found a shady spot and tried not to get too nervous about watching him conquer some tricky cornice or something. Why are you asking about climbing?"

He trusted her, he thought again. She deserved to know the direction the investigation was taking them. "Can you come outside with me to take a look at something?"

She looked puzzled but rose immediately and followed him out the back door and around the side of the house toward Cameron's bedroom.

"You told Sheriff Galvez the alarm system was set and the dead bolt was locked on the outside doors, correct?" he asked as they walked.

"Yes."

"Are you positive about that?"

"Absolutely. I double-checked them when I woke up, before I found Cam missing. I always do when I wake up in the night. I'm still a city girl at heart, I guess."

"If that's true, the only other exit is out the window. You told the sheriff that when you found Cameron wasn't in bed the window was open but the screen was in place, right?"

"That's right."

"The state crime scene detective has determined the screen was in backward, as if someone replaced it from the outside. That's consistent with the window-as-exit-route theory, but we can't find any evidence on the ground of ladder impressions. It's always a possibility the rain may have washed it away. Or Cameron may have taken another route down."

"Like what?"

He pointed to the discovery he'd made earlier with Wilhelmina Carson. "Take a look at those holes there. What do they look like?'"

She frowned. "I don't know. Termites?"

He caught his smile before it could even start. If those were termite holes, the whole house was in serious trouble. "Look at how uniformly round they are, and the placement of them."

She stuck a finger in the lowest one, the same one he had used to launch upward. "I'm sorry. I don't understand."

He sighed, his shoulder already crying out in protest at what he knew he would have to demonstrate again. He slipped off his shoes and socks again and used the finger holes to scale the wall, stopping a few lengths below where he'd climbed with Willy.

When he dropped to the ground, she stared at him as if he had just stripped naked and cartwheeled across her flower garden.

"You can't honestly believe Cam used those tiny holes to climb out of a second-story window?"

"The crime scene investigator dusted for prints. She found several sets of prints inside the holes. All of them consistent with what we believe are Cam's from the evidence in his bedroom."

"He's nine years old, for heaven's sake. And small for his age!"

"How much climbing experience has he had?"

She shivered, though the hot wind still blew out of the mountains. "Some. Okay, quite a bit. We had vaulted ceilings in our house in San Diego and Rick…Rick built a climbing wall in the playroom. Cam loved it, probably because it made him feel closer to his father."

She stared at those holes, her delicate features troubled. "Suppose I buy your theory that he climbed out of his room on his own. Why on earth would he do such a thing in the middle of the night? Where would he go? Cam didn't have friends around except his cousins. He wasn't happy about moving away from San Diego, but he had no reason to run away!"

Her voice broke on the last word, and her struggle for control was painful to witness.

He didn't know what to say, hesitant to offer her false hope, so he opted to change the subject.

"Have you eaten anything today?" he asked. "You should keep your strength up."

"Why does everyone seem to think all I need to do is eat to survive this horrible experience? I've heard those same words from half a dozen people today."

"Sorry. Habit, I guess."

She sighed. "No, I'm sorry. I'm not hungry right now. I'll have time to eat after my son is in my arms again."

He had no answer to that and could only hope she wouldn't starve to death waiting for her son.

"Cameron will be home again, Agent Davis," she said, her voice wavering only a little. "I know it in my gut. I don't care how many cases you've worked on that have ended badly. This one won't. It *won't*."

I hope you're right, he thought, but couldn't bring himself to say the words as they walked back into the house.

6:22 p.m.

"Great green globs of greasy grimy gopher guts, dadda, dadda dadda da, dadda dadda dadda da. Great green globs of greasy grimy gopher guts and I forgot my spooooooooon."

His voice wobbled a little on the last word of the Boy Scout song he'd learned from his cousin Nate, but since there was nobody around to hear, Cameron didn't do anything to hide it.

This was about his zillionth time through that stupid song and he still couldn't remember all the words. Still, singing it kind of helped him keep the panic away and not feel so alone in here.

He was so turned around now, he didn't have the first idea which way to go.

His cousin was an Eagle Scout and right then he would have given anything to be able to ask Nate what he should do.

When they used to go on fishing trips and stuff, his dad taught him that if he was ever lost in the mountains, he should just stay put until somebody found him. But he knew he couldn't do that in here since nobody would even know where to start looking for him.

He didn't want to die.

He'd been worrying about that more and more as the hours went by. After his dad was killed, he had hurt so much and missed him so bad he thought he wanted to.

He still missed him and it still hurt thinking about all the fun stuff they used to do together. But he still had Hailey and Mom. They would be really sad if he died in here, and he didn't want his mom to cry anymore.

There were too many other things he would miss if he died. Spitting watermelon seeds off the back step with Hailey. Lying on the trampoline in the backyard with his mom, counting the stars. Heck, this weekend was the Moosemania parade and carnival, and Nate promised he would ride the Vomit Comet with him, which sounded totally cool.

If he died, he could never be an Eagle Scout like his cousin and he would never be able to learn the other words to that dumb song.

Somewhere in the distance, he suddenly heard a loud creak, then a rumble. That was about the third time he'd heard a noise like that. At first, he thought the whole mine was going to collapse but now he figured it was just the earth settling a little.

He took one more bite of granola bar, then stowed it back in his pack and turned on his flashlight again. He was down to one spare set of batteries and he was going to have to use them soon since these were getting dim.

More tired than he'd ever been in his life, Cam stood up and forced himself to keep going. The walls were tight here and he felt like toothpaste squeezing through a tube, but when he shined the wavering beam of the light ahead, he could see the passageway open up a little more. Just a little farther now.

The batteries died when he was just about through the tight part. Since there wasn't room to maneuver his pack out and change them, he decided to press on until the passage widened.

He hated the total darkness but he forced himself to go forward. Another foot, then another, each step taking him closer to his mom and his sister.

He hoped, anyway.

He breathed a sigh of relief when he felt the passageway widen. Just a little farther now and then he would stop and change his flashlight batteries.

He put his left foot forward but to his horror, he hit nothing but air. A vertical shaft! He tried to pull his foot back to solid ground but felt the dirt and rocks on the edge of the shaft break loose under his boots. He had nothing to hang on to, nothing to keep him from pitching forward down into emptiness.

He screamed as he fell, and then the world went black.

Chapter 5

"So far we've got a whole lot of nothing." Gage sighed. "No prints, no trace, no evidence whatsoever that anybody forced Cameron Vance out of his bed. By all appearances, it looks like the boy left on his own, especially given the fingerholes you found and the absence of any other fingerprints in them but his. My canvass of the neighbors has turned up exactly nothing. Everyone was sound asleep in their beds after midnight."

They sat in a corner of the huge tent awning set up near the mobile command center for volunteers to rest and eat. A sandwich shop in town had donated enough food to feed a small army, and Cale and his partner were exchanging information over subs.

So much for the advice he had given Megan about eating to keep up strength. This was his first nourishment since they had arrived on the scene more than twelve hours ago.

He wasn't hungry, either, but he forced himself to eat, knowing he might not have a chance for twelve more hours.

"But what happened to him after he left the house? That's the question," Cale responded. "The search dogs haven't picked up jack, and there's no trace of the kid anywhere. If he did climb out that window, we have no idea which direction he headed in once he hit the ground."

"Those mountains are pretty vast. My guess is he's somewhere up there. I only hope the searchers can get a bead on him before nightfall. Even though it's hotter than hell right now, you know how the temperature drops in these mountains after the sun goes down. I hate the idea of any little kid having to spend a cold night alone in those hills, and especially one with a fragile medical condition."

Gage always was a sucker for a kid in trouble but since his marriage and entry into instant fatherhood three years earlier, he had become even more empathetic.

Cale wouldn't have expected it, but Gage had really taken to fatherhood after marrying a widow with two little girls. His wife Allie had given birth to a boy a few years earlier and the McKinnon family was warm and loving and happy.

Cale wasn't sure how his partner pulled it off, working among the dregs of society all day, then going home to his sweet wife and kids at night. But somehow Gage made it work. He was one of the best fathers Cale had ever known and his marriage had somehow made him even better at his job, with a new dedication and focus.

"Megan says he's a tough kid," Cale responded. "He must be if he was able to climb out the window and make it to the ground using only three-quarter-inch finger holes."

Gage gave him a quizzical look. "Megan?"

"Mrs. Vance," he corrected, though he had been thinking of her by her first name for several hours now.

His partner continued to study him, and Cale decided he didn't like having that analytical gaze aimed in his direction.

"I don't know how much longer we'll be working this case. You know that, don't you?" his partner said after a moment.

Cale nodded, though he didn't want to think about it. With no evidence of foul play coming to light to date, this case appeared to fall squarely under the sheriff's jurisdiction.

"When I briefed Curtis an hour ago, he was already making noises about pulling us in, questioning whether we should even be here or should turn our notes over to the local authorities."

He wasn't ready to give up looking for the boy. Somehow over the course of the day, this case had become about far more than just doing his job. "Curtis is a horse's ass."

McKinnon made a face. "Careful there. He's still your boss."

"Acting boss," he muttered. "Only until next month, when Moyer gets back from training in Quantico."

"In the meantime, we've got to do our best to play by Curtis's rules. And right now he's questioning our presence on a case that by all appearances looks like a kid who ran away looking for a little adventure and maybe got lost in the mountains. He's very cognizant that we've got no evidence to indicate otherwise."

"What we've got is a missing kid with a life-threatening seizure condition. Until we know for sure nobody else was involved in his disappearance, I'm not going anywhere."

McKinnon blinked a little at the force of his conviction, but to Cale's immense relief his partner said nothing. They continued their briefing, finished their sandwiches, then rose to return to work.

Cale must have stood too abruptly. His rickety folding chair started to topple backward and he instinctively reached to catch it, jarring his shoulder in the process.

He winced as pain scorched through him, then instantly regretted it when McKinnon made a sound of disgust.

"You need to take it easy, man."

"I'm fine," he insisted. He was, for the most part. As gunshot wounds go, this one had been relatively clean. He had lost a great deal of blood, but the bullet only took a chunk out of his collarbone and lodged in his deltoid muscle.

It still hurt like hell sometimes, but only when he overdid it. He supposed scaling halfway up a two-story wall using only fingerholes might qualify as overdoing it. Doing it twice was probably bordering on insane.

"Allie's going to kill me for dragging you out here before you were ready to be back on the job."

Cale shook his head. "I was ready. More than ready. I don't need more time to sit around and think."

He didn't want or need the compassion in his partner's gaze. "You can't tell me you're a hundred percent yet."

"Can't I?" he muttered.

"Not with any chance in hell of me believing you. How long have we been partners? Going on four years now, right?"

"Something like that."

"There have been some cases in that time that have messed with both our heads. CAC can be a tough assignment." He was quiet. "But since everything went down two weeks ago, there's a wildness in you I've never seen before."

"Drop it, McKinnon. I'm fine."

As usual, his partner ignored him. "I know you went through hell trying to save those girls, Cale. Everybody knows that. You need to give yourself a break. You did the best you could."

He was getting damn sick and tired of everybody telling him that. If he *had* done the best he could, people would have no reason to say the words because Soshi and Mirabel would still be alive.

"Why don't you take a few more days?" Gage went on. "I can handle this case on my own."

"The case nobody thinks we have?"

"Yeah. That one." McKinnon smiled but there was more worry than humor in it. "We're bound to get a break soon. The kid couldn't have completely vanished. Maybe when the sun goes down and that bitch of a wind dies, the dogs will pick something up."

He hoped so. He didn't relish watching Megan Vance endure a night without her child.

"Where do you think we should go from here?" he asked when they walked out of the sweltering mess tent into the even more punishing wind.

"I thought I would comb through the list of registered sex offenders in the area again and see if anything new jumps out. Why don't you get an update from Daniel Galvez on the search progress?"

He nodded and they both headed toward the house. They were a few dozen yards away when the screen door banged shut and Megan Vance rushed out the door.

And McKinnon thought *he* had a wildness to him now. Megan looked completely frantic suddenly, her eyes huge and shadowed in her pale, delicate features.

He hurried forward without any conscious awareness of it and before he realized exactly how it happened she sagged against him, collapsing in his arms.

"What is it, Megan?"

"Where is he? Why can't they find him? Something's wrong. We've got to hurry!"

He set her away from him, gripping her elbows. "Slow down. What happened to upset you?"

She took several deep breaths and he watched her struggle for control. Some of her hysteria began to fade.

"I don't know. I was in the kitchen talking on the phone to one of the neighbors and suddenly this horrible, black feeling just seemed to ooze through me. He's hurt. I know he is. I don't know how I know, but I do. My baby is somewhere hurt and he needs his mother and I'm stuck here doing absolutely nothing to find him!"

She started to weep. Cale couldn't help himself; he pulled her back into his arms, concerned only with offering the small comfort he could provide.

"I'm so terrified," she sobbed. "He's so little and it's going to be dark soon. I can't bear to think of him out there by himself somewhere."

"I know. I know."

He had no words of solace to offer her. She would recognize anything he had to say for exactly what it was—meaningless, empty platitudes. He could only continue to let her lean against him, completely ignoring the discomfort to his shoulder.

He didn't think Megan even knew his partner was still there. She certainly didn't seem to even notice when McKinnon gave him an odd look then, blessedly, disappeared into the house.

They stood for a long time in the hot swirl of wind while she sobbed and he tried like hell to fight the tenderness stirring to life inside him.

He didn't want it. He couldn't afford to let this woman with her troubles into his life, to let himself begin to care about Megan Vance and her missing son.

Maybe it would be better if they *were* pulled off this case. He was losing all objectivity here and wanted fiercely to make everything all better for her, something he knew was completely out of his power.

After a moment she stepped away, rubbing at her eyes with the same handkerchief he'd given her hours earlier. "I'm...I'm sorry to break down like this. I've tried to be strong all day but I just...I'm afraid I lost it."

"Don't apologize. You're dealing with incredible levels of stress most of us can't begin to understand."

"I'm not crazy, even though I must have seemed like it. Something happened to him. I know he's hurt somewhere. As I said, I don't know how I know but I do. We have to find him."

"We're trying, Megan. You must believe everyone out there is doing all they can, from Sheriff Galvez to the search and rescue team to the volunteers. We all want the same thing you do, to see your son back home."

"I know."

She started to add something more but before she could, the screen door banged again and her sister hurried down the steps, accompanied by a little girl with long red braids and freckles.

Even if he hadn't seen Hailey Vance's picture throughout the house, he would have known she was Megan's daughter. The resemblance between them was startling.

"Mommy!" the little girl exclaimed, pulling her hand from her aunt's and rushing to her mother.

Megan knelt to her daughter's level and folded her into a tight hug, her eyes closed. Some of the tension seemed to seep out of her as she held the girl close for a long moment.

"I'm sorry," Molly Randall murmured. "After dinner, she wanted her mommy and no one else would do. I thought it might lift your spirits to see her before I settle her for the night."

"It does," Megan smiled at her sister, then turned back to Hailey. "It's so good to see you, sweetheart. What have you been doing today?"

"Me and Kenna played Barbies and went swimming and Nate put the sprinkler under the trampoline and we jumped through it. I didn't have my suit, so I had to wear Kenna's."

"That sounds fun," Megan answered. "We'll find your suit so you can take it back with you."

"Okay."

"What else have you done?"

Her brow furrowed as she tried to remember. "Well,

we had melty cheese sandwiches for lunch and lots of people have been coming with food and stuff. Kenna says they're just trying to help find Cam. But I don't see how a tuna casserole can do that."

Megan's mouth lifted into a semblance of a smile, and he was struck again by how fragile and lovely she seemed, even under these terrible circumstances.

"When people are having a hard time, their neighbors like to help with food. Sometimes when they don't know what else to do, they bring food over so they can nourish the body along with lifting spirits."

"I think it's nice."

Megan smoothed a hand down her daughter's bedraggled braid. "I do, too, sweetheart."

With an odd catch in his chest, Cale decided his presence was no longer needed. She had her family around her to help buoy her up and he had work to do.

He turned to leave, but the girl caught sight of him before he could escape.

"Hi." She smiled shyly. "I'm Hailey Marie Vance. I'm six."

She held out a small hand for him to shake and he had no choice but to comply.

Suddenly his breathing felt tight and his blood pulsed loudly in his ears. She was six years old, the same age as Mirabel Decker. As he looked at Megan's daughter, for a moment all he could think about was how much blood could spill out of a tiny frame this size.

He pushed away the images that haunted him and forced a smile. "Hi, Hailey. I'm Caleb Davis. I'm thirty-five."

"That's old."

He decided she probably wouldn't understand if he told her he felt older by the moment.

Before he could summon an answer, her mother made an embarrassed sound. "Hailey, it's rude to tell people they're old. And thirty-five is not old, just older than you."

"I'm sorry." When she smiled at him so sweetly, Cale knew he would forgive her just about anything.

"No problem," he said brusquely, to hide the sudden tumult of his emotions.

"Are you helping to find my brother?"

"We're trying."

"Thank you." She reached a hand out again and slipped it through his, squeezing tightly, and Cale almost thought he could hear a deep, hollow thud as he tumbled into love with this sweet little girl.

He had to clear his throat before he could answer. "You're welcome. It was nice to meet you, Hailey Marie Vance."

She smiled at him again and in that moment, he knew it wouldn't matter if Curtis pulled them off the job. No matter what happened, he wasn't going to walk away from this case until Cameron Vance was home with his mother.

He had vacation time and medical leave remaining, and he would use every last bit of it if he had to.

He didn't have a choice here. Somehow in the course of twelve hours, this case had become more to him than simply another missing child.

"I like your FBI agent."

Megan froze in the act of folding Hailey's favorite pair of pajamas. She set them carefully in the suitcase

along with her swimsuit and extra playclothes for the
next day and tried hard not to look at her sister.

"He's not *my* FBI agent."

Molly raised an eyebrow and Megan flushed, remembering the way she had rushed straight into his arms.

How could she have let her emotions swell out of
control that way? She still wasn't sure what had set her
off earlier, but she still couldn't shake this niggling
urgency that Cam was hurt somewhere.

She also had no idea why she had turned so instantly
to a hardened FBI agent she had barely met—or why his
whipcord-lean frame had come to represent such comfort.

"He has kind eyes," Molly went on, "though they certainly look like they've seen things I can't even imagine.
And did you catch how oddly he reacted to Hailey?"

She *had* noticed his odd response. For an instant, she
thought she had almost seen a look of anguish in the
polar-blue depths of his eyes, though now she wondered
if she had imagined the whole thing.

"What did you say his name was?" Molly asked.

"Davis. Cale Davis."

"That name seems familiar." She frowned. "Wait,
isn't he the one..."

Her voice suddenly trailed off and she jerked her
gaze back to the cartload of toys she was trying to stuff
into the small suitcase. "Um, never mind."

Megan glared at her sister. "I hate it when you do
that. Isn't he *what* one?"

Molly shrugged, looking troubled. "An FBI agent
was injured a few weeks ago. I saw it on TV. I wondered
if it might be him, but I'm sure I must be mistaken."

Was she? It would make sense, with some of the

undercurrents she had caught between him and his partner. And she had noticed several times during their various interactions how he seemed to hold his left arm a little more stiffly than the right.

How had he been injured? she wondered. And under what circumstances that might have put that bleak look in his eyes?

He wasn't the sort who invited confidences. He was a hard man in a dangerous profession, and she would be wise to keep that in mind.

Caleb Davis wasn't an easy, comfortable kind of man. She had no idea how he could develop a skin tough enough to work in the midst of overwhelming grief and pain and horror day after day without it piercing his soul.

Or maybe it had. Maybe that raw emotion in his eyes she thought she had glimpsed indicated his skin wasn't as impervious as she might have expected.

"Mommy, I can't decide which doll to take." Hailey broke into her thoughts by tossing two dolls on her lap. "Samantha is the pretty one, but Holly Hobbie is soft to cuddle when I'm sad."

She was grateful for the interruption, she thought. She far preferred focusing on her bright and loving child than on FBI agents with secrets in their eyes.

"Why don't you take both?" she suggested. "Then you don't have to decide."

Hailey reacted to the simple suggestion with glee and beamed as if her mother were a genius.

Megan had decided a long time ago that was one of the best things about being a mother. At least when they were young, her children thought she could do no wrong. At nine, Cameron was fast growing out of that phase, at least judging by how upset he had been at her for moving him from San Diego, but Hailey still thought she was brilliant.

After they packed Hailey's little pink suitcase and loaded Daisy's cage, Megan walked her sister and daughter to Molly's Expedition, parked in front of the house. The sun was beginning to sink below the horizon, and long purple shadows extended across her property.

The hot wind seemed to be dying down as the sun began to set. She wanted to be grateful for that— perhaps the search dogs might be able to pick up a scent now. At the same time, as the sun set, the temperature dropped and her son was still out there.

She pushed her fears aside for now, focusing on the routine act of strapping Hailey in the seat belt. When she was secure, she planted a big kiss on her daughter's forehead. "You be good for Aunt Molly and Uncle Scott and have fun sleeping in McKenna's room."

"Okay, Mommy. Will Cameron be home when I wake up?"

"Oh, I hope so, sweetheart." She mustered a smile, though she felt as if her skin would crack apart from the effort.

She closed the door, then leaned into Molly's open window to press her cheek to her sister's. "Thank you for everything," she murmured to Molly. "I couldn't survive this without you."

"You're my baby sister. I just wish I could make it all better for you." Molly's chin quivered and tears brimmed in her eyes, but she blinked them away. "Take care of yourself. I'll come back up once the kids are in bed and Scott comes back from searching."

She wanted to tell her sister she didn't need her, but she had never been good at lying to Molly so she just nodded.

Chapter 6

7:15 p.m.

Cameron woke slowly, painfully.

He didn't know where he was at first, or why he felt as if he had just spent an hour tossing around in a clothes dryer. Why was he lying here in the dirt, whimpering like a baby for his mom? And why was it so dark?

He blinked a few times and awareness slithered over him like his friend Joey's pet snake.

In a blink he remembered it all—his excitement at the adventure the night before, then the horror when it all went so terribly wrong, then the long hours of wandering to find his way out again.

He had fallen, he remembered. A vertical shaft opened up and he slipped down. How far had he tumbled? It couldn't have been too far, or he would be in heaven with his dad by now.

He sat up, aware of the back of his head throbbing like the time he had a toothache and had to get a cavity filled. If it hurt this bad even with his bike helmet on, how much worse would it have been if he hadn't been wearing it?

What else had he hurt? He tried to move everything to see if he'd broken any bones. When he straightened his legs, burning pain shot up from both knees. A whimper escaped him but he cut it off as he reached down and found his pants had ripped in the fall. He brushed away tiny pebbles and who knew what else.

His hand came away wet and he figured out the knee that hurt the most must be bleeding.

In his backpack he had a small first aid kit, he remembered. He reached for it, but his hands came away empty. It wasn't there!

He suddenly felt as if he'd eaten a whole peanut butter sandwich in one bite without a glass of milk, as if he were choking on the panic. His pack! All his supplies—his extra flashlight, the last set of batteries, his granola bars. Everything was gone.

He tried the flashlight still hooked around his neck by the lanyard. It put out a burst of light for about half a second, then sputtered and died. The batteries had gone out on the level above, he remembered, when he had been squeezing through that tight area. That's why he hadn't seen the vertical drop until it was too late.

He had to find his pack. He *had* to. He would never survive in here in the dark without it.

Sobbing with fear, he crawled around on hands and

knees, exploring the space around him in hopes of finding something. He had to ignore the sharp pain in his knees and palms, but at last—just when he had just about given up hope—his left hand encountered something soft and wet.

He clutched it to him with a sob of relief. Why was it wet, though? He quickly discovered the answer to that. Almost all his extra water bottles had leaked in the fall, drenching just about everything in the pack.

There was a little bit left in one, and he still had a little less than half of the other one. He could only hope that would be enough, and that the batteries weren't ruined.

Working as fast as he could, he found the last two batteries and fumbled in the pitch darkness to put them into the flashlight the correct way. When the beam immediately came on, he cried and laughed at the same time.

The first thing he checked was how far he had fallen. He shined the light up and saw it must have been only about eight or nine feet.

He was really lucky. There were vertical shafts in here that were much deeper than that. But how was he going to get back up to the level that he knew would take him out?

Could he climb it? he wondered. The dirt and rocks around the shaft weren't exactly stable, but he would have to try.

He didn't have any choice.

It took him almost an hour and he fell back down twice, but at long last he managed to pull himself back to the top of the shaft. He flopped down on the tunnel floor, not sure what was making him shake—the hunger pangs in his stomach, the pain in his head, or his fear.

Cam didn't think he had ever been so tired. He was going to have to rest before he tried to go on—he had been up since midnight when he started to get ready to leave, and only had a few hours of sleep before that.

He let himself have what was left in the water bottle that had mostly spilled out and took two bites of his granola bar. He felt better after that.

He should probably try to sleep a little, he decided. He would have to, or he would risk making another stupid mistake like walking straight into a vertical shaft.

He pulled out the survival blanket, rolled up in it and huddled against the wall of the tunnel. He would rest for a little while, then he would see what he could do about getting the heck out of here.

"You sure you wouldn't rather come home with me to Park City for the night?" Gage McKinnon asked.

It was almost 11:00 p.m. and most of the searchers had been sent home for the night to rest and recharge, though the command center still bustled with activity as coordinators tried to map out the search grid for the next day.

"I can guarantee my guest room is a whole lot more comfortable than some stretch of floor somewhere in the middle of a search operation," Gage went on.

Cale shook his head. "Thanks for the offer, but I feel better about crashing here, just in case anything breaks in the night."

His partner raised an eyebrow. "You can be back in Moose Springs from my place in half an hour. Come on, you know Allie's going to skin me alive if I let you sleep on the floor somewhere when you're barely two weeks away from a gunshot wound."

"What your lovely and compassionate wife doesn't know won't hurt her. She's got enough on her hands with the girls and Toby and managing her diabetes. She doesn't need to babysit me, too."

At the mention of his family, Gage smiled softly, as he always did, and Cale was surprised at the envy that suddenly gouged him like sharp claws in the gut.

Where the hell had that come from? he wondered.

He had always considered himself content with his life and had long ago decided the whole wife-and-kids scene wasn't for him.

He wasn't cut out to be a husband and father. He had cohabited with a woman exactly one time, a six-week trial about eight years earlier that had been disastrous all the way around. He made a lousy partner, at least in any nonprofessional capacity. He liked not having to report his whereabouts if he decided to head off to the canyons above the city for some rock climbing. He liked sleeping on whichever the hell side of the bed he wanted. With no one to nag him—except McKinnon, anyway—he could work as long as he wanted and could pour all his energy into the job.

That was the life he preferred, the one he had carved out for himself. Besides his own personal preference, he had absolutely no idea how to make a successful family life, not with a childhood that ranked somewhere between grossly dysfunctional and sheer purgatory.

But just now, the thought of having someone warm and sweet waiting at home to help him through the tough days, to hold him tight and help him forget for a while, seemed incredibly appealing.

"Why don't you at least stay out at the Bittercreek

with Mason and Jane?" Gage pressed. "They're only five minutes away."

His friend Mason and his wife Jane were as deliriously happy together as Gage and his wife. Of all the men he might have expected to fall hard one day, the tough-as-cowhide ex-spy Cale had met through investigating a covert child-smuggling operation in southeast Asia would have been last on the list.

But Gage was completely smitten with his British wife and the two Filipino children they had adopted. He had walked away from The Game without a backward glance and now seemed to want nothing else but to raise horses and kids on the same ranch where he'd grown up.

"I talked to Mason a few hours ago," he told Gage. "He offered their guest room, too, but I feel better staying here, just in case."

McKinnon shook his head. "You are one stubborn SOB."

"So they tell me."

At the door, his partner scrutinized him carefully. "This case is under your skin, isn't it?"

Big-time. He knew the Bureau shrink he was supposed to see since the Decker debacle would probably give this some fancy name, would tell him he had some kind of messianic complex or something. He only knew it had become vitally important for him to find Cameron Vance, in a way he didn't quite understand.

"More than anything, I'm baffled by it."

"It is a strange one, that's for sure."

"I can't figure out why the boy would just take off like that in the middle of the night. He just doesn't strike me as the kind of kid to cut and run."

"Kids get crazy ideas. I should know. Gaby and Anna keep us running every minute to keep up with them."

"But Cameron Vance's whole dream is to be Special Forces, even given his medical condition. He idolizes his father's memory and spent a lot of time with the other men in his dad's unit. I'm positive he knows a SEAL wouldn't just suddenly ditch his problems and hit the road."

"I have to tell you, I'm not convinced someone else wasn't involved. Maybe someone close to the kid has gone to a lot of trouble to make it look like Cameron climbed out of his bedroom on his own."

"It wasn't his mother," he said sharply.

Gage raised an eyebrow. "I didn't say it was. I still can't shake the possibility that even though we only found his fingerprints in those holes, someone could have been waiting for him on the ground."

He hated even thinking about it. "You figure out who that might be and where they might have gone with him so we can bring him home and all go home."

"We're working as hard as we can on this, Cale. What do you think you're going to accomplish for the kid pulling an all-nighter, especially in your condition?"

Probably nothing. He knew that, but he just couldn't make himself leave yet.

"Go home and get some rest. I'll see you in the morning," he said instead of answering.

McKinnon shook his head. "One stubborn SOB," he repeated, but to Cale's relief he didn't push him anymore.

After his partner left, Cale decided to go in search of Daniel Galvez for an update on what areas had been searched that day and where the grid would take them in the morning.

He walked out into the cool night air, noticing the flare of flashlights moving slowly on the mountains as the search dog team worked. At the mobile command center, he pushed open the door and found only a handful of people inside, including the man he had come looking for.

The sheriff gave him a startled look out of red-rimmed, tired-looking eyes. "Davis! I thought I saw you FBI boys leave for the night."

"Gage went back to his house in Park City to catch some sleep. I thought I'd stick around, if you have no objection."

"None at all. I'm glad you're here. Save me the trouble of tracking you down. We've got a lead that's probably not connected to Cameron, but it bears looking into."

"Yeah?"

The sheriff pulled a paper out of the fax machine. "One of my deputies just took another missing persons report. High school dropout by the name of Wally Simon. One of our regulars. We've busted him half a dozen times since he turned eighteen last year. Petty stuff mostly, though my deputies like to keep their eyes on him. He lives with his mother, Enid, who said he disappeared a week or so ago. She's worried he might be mixed up with something over his head."

"She give any specifics?"

"She says a few weeks ago he seemed to come into some money but wouldn't tell her where he got it."

"Drugs?"

"It's possible. Kid's a pothead. I can easily see him growing a stash somewhere in the mountains."

"Any connection you're aware of between him and our missing boy?" Cale asked.

"Not that I know about. But I should tell you, Simon's a climber when he's not high. He bored everybody in town for months last year bragging about the fourteener he climbed in Colorado. He sometimes hangs out at the climbing wall in town where Nate Randall works."

Cale digested this new information, sifting through it to try to come up with some kind of link he could work with.

He hated to ask but had no choice. "Would this Simon be the sort to show up on your radar as a possible child predator?"

The sheriff scratched his chin. He looked like a man in need of sleep and a good shave, and Cale felt a pang of sympathy for him.

Moose Springs wasn't big on crime. He imagined two missing persons cases in one day would put a serious strain on the resources of the small-town sheriff's department.

"My gut says no. Simon's a little prick with a substance-abuse problem and a bad attitude, but none of his past collars have been for anything of a sexual nature that might indicate something like that."

He would have to check it out, regardless. "Would I be stepping on any toes if I talked to the mother?"

"You can certainly try. She didn't say much to my deputy, other than to report his disappearance."

"I don't suppose you have a ride I can borrow? My partner left with our department vehicle."

Galvez sighed. "Take mine. I'm not going anywhere tonight."

* * *

It was close to 1:00 a.m. when he returned to the Vance log home, frustrated and out of sorts. The lead had gone nowhere, just as he might have predicted. Enid Simon had been not only uncooperative but close to obstructive.

She refused to tell him the names of any of her son's friends and wouldn't let him take a look at Wally's room or the piece-of-crap junker he drove that was still parked in the driveway of their dilapidated trailer. She only scoffed when he asked her if her son might have any connection to nine-year-old Cameron Vance.

It was a big waste of two hours, as far as he was concerned. When he returned to the Vance property, he reported the fruitless interview to an unsurprised Sheriff Galvez.

"There's nothing more you can do here tonight," Daniel said. "Get some rest. We've got a cot in the back of the command center nobody's using. You're welcome to crash there."

"You mind if I take a look at the boy's room one more time? I keep thinking there's something we're missing here."

"Yeah, I feel the same way," the sheriff said. "My guys are killing themselves looking for this boy and we're coming up with absolutely nothing. I hope you find something because I sure as hell don't know where to turn."

Inside the house, he found the crime unit had finished its job and taped up the door. Cale could have moved it aside and entered, but he only reached inside to switch on the light and surveyed the room from the hall.

With the soccer ball comforter on the bed and the

wadded-up clothes on the floor, it seemed like a typical boy's bedroom, except for the shrine to Captain Rick Vance on the wall.

He focused his attention closer on the picture in the middle of all the military honors.

Vance had brown hair and wasn't smiling. He might have looked stern, except for a telltale gleam in his blue eyes. It could have been laughter or excitement or maybe just plain old enjoyment of life.

He looked like a hell-raiser, like one of those neck-or-nothing types who tried to reach out with both hands to grab everything life had to offer him.

Cale had the strange thought that he probably would have liked the man if he'd ever had the chance to meet him.

Now, he only felt a deep pity that Rick Vance had missed out on watching his children grow up, on cuddling his pretty wife on a rainy spring night, on coaching his son's soccer team and walking his beautiful daughter down the aisle.

The sudden soft swirl of vanilla and cinnamon gave him his first warning he wasn't alone.

"Rick's death hit Cam hard," a quiet voice interrupted his thoughts. "Maybe harder than I realized. He adored his father."

He turned to find Megan standing a few feet away, following his gaze. She looked fragile and pale, her eyes tired and inexpressibly sad. He was taken aback by the ferocity of his sudden urge to fit her close to him and try to soak up some of this burden for her.

He fisted one hand against the wood of the door frame and shoved the other into his pocket to keep from surrendering to the impulse.

"I didn't expect you to be here tonight," he said gently. "You need to get some rest. Why didn't you go to your sister's house, somewhere away from this for a while?"

She shrugged. "I can't leave," she said simply. "What if they find him in the night and he needs me? I have to be here."

How many nights would she have to cling to that faith? He hoped to God it wasn't many.

"I could say the same for you," she said. "I thought I saw your partner leave some time ago. I was certain you must have left with him. Why are you still here?"

He couldn't very well verbalize something he didn't fully understand himself. "I figured one of us should stick around if something broke in the case during the night," he said, which was at least part of the truth. "There's a cot in the mobile command unit. I'll crash there in a while."

"Not much is happening tonight. I know they've sent most of the searchers home to rest."

"The dogs are still out there."

"I know. I also know that with every moment that passes, Cameron's scent becomes harder and harder for the dogs to find."

She said the words with a grim fatalism that broke his heart, especially as he could provide absolutely nothing positive for her to hang on to.

Hoping to distract her, he turned his attention to the pictures hanging in the hallway. She had turned it into a family gallery of sorts, mostly of the children at various ages, but a few looked to be of the whole family before Captain Vance's death.

In one, they stood at the railing of a boat in what he

guessed to be San Diego Harbor. In another, Rick Vance sat on a beach with both his children on his lap. Still another was of Vance and his son alone, posing at the mouth of a cave.

He paused at that one, recognizing the setting. "That's Timpanogas Cave in Utah County, isn't it?"

She nodded with a small smile of remembrance. "Right before Rick's unit was sent on their second tour to Afghanistan, a few months before his death, we came to Utah to visit Molly and Scott. Scott and Rick took the kids up there one day and Cam loved it. He talked about it for weeks."

He was touched by the way her features lit up when she talked about her son. "You didn't go along?" he asked.

"It was one of those father-son bonding moments. Besides, Hailey was only two at the time, and Rick and I both decided we didn't want to lug her up the mountainside. And I'm better on solid ground anyway. I think I told you I'm not very crazy about heights."

"They look like they're having a great time."

"That's not my favorite picture of their trip. I've got a scrapbook downstairs, if you would like to see it."

He sensed more in her words than just an invitation for him to look through family pictures. She needed to talk about her son, if only to shore up her flagging spirits.

Even if he could do nothing else to find her son tonight, he could at least listen to her.

Chapter 7

In the large, comfortable two-story great room, Megan went immediately to a wall of built-in bookshelves near the river-rock fireplace and pulled out a three-inch-thick book with a leather binding.

"Here it is. This is Cameron's life in pictures." She smiled a little. "I've been keeping it for him since he was born. This one is almost full. I guess it's time to start a new one. I'll have plenty of newspaper clippings to put in that one after we find him."

He envied her her faith, more so because he knew how hard she fought to cling to it.

She perched on the edge of the leather sofa and he joined her, waiting while she thumbed through the pictures in the book until she found the one she wanted. "Here we go. This is my favorite. Rick took it."

It was a picture of Cameron alone, a towheaded boy

with his mother's eyes and his father's mouth and freckles scattered across his nose and cheekbones.

He sat on a huge granite boulder with his hands grasping his upraised knees, looking at the vast valley spread out beneath him as if a world of possibilities waited for him below.

He had to be only six or so in the pictures, barely past preschool, but there was a solemn maturity in his eyes that Cale found a little disconcerting. Perhaps the boy's epilepsy gave him wisdom beyond his years. Or perhaps he had some child's intuition of the pain of his father's death he would have to endure shortly.

"He talked about that trip for months. I promised him we'd make it back up there after we moved back to Utah but we've been so busy settling in, I haven't had a chance." Her voice broke a little on the last word.

"Timpanogas is a cool cave," he said after a moment, giving her time to regain control. "I hiked up there once when I was in college."

She blinked away her tears, as he had hoped she would. After a moment she swallowed and responded. "Are you from Utah, then? For some reason, I wouldn't have expected you to be a native."

Big mistake, bringing up his own past. He never quite knew how to answer that question, how to explain the complex, twisting road he had traveled to this point in his life.

"I grew up in a tiny dot on the map in southern Utah until I was twelve but I lived in the Ogden area through high school and went to college at the University of Utah."

It was carefully worded truth, as all his statements about his past had to be, but left out a few major details.

Most people tended to get a little jumpy if he told them he spent a year at the Moweda juvenile detention facility and the rest of his youth in foster care.

He usually solved that pesky issue by not revealing anything about his past.

"Do you have family around, then?"

"No. No family."

He wasn't sure what made him say it, maybe the intimacy of the night or some need to let her know he wasn't unfamiliar with pain, but before he realized it, he told her the one detail only Gage knew about him. "I had a sister, but she died the year I turned twelve."

The year his whole life went to hell.

No, that wasn't strictly true. It had felt like it at the time, but looking back, he could see his life had already been hell before that terrible time. In an odd, twisted way, Jerusha's death had set him free.

He never would have expected the darkest time in his life would eventually give way to something he had never once known in twelve years of misery.

Hope.

"I'm sorry."

Her expressive green eyes filled with sympathy. He couldn't believe that even in the midst of her own nightmare, Megan could find room to share his pain.

"Was she ill?" she asked.

Now that he had given her the bare bones of information, he knew he would have to fill in the details, no matter how painful.

"She killed herself," he finally said.

Her hand reached out to grasp his fingers. "Oh, Cale. I'm so sorry. You were twelve?"

"Right. Jerusha was fourteen." He couldn't seem to look away from their entwined fingers, wondering why they made his eyes burn and his chest feel so tight.

He had told her that much. He might as well tell her the rest. "We didn't have it easy as kids. Our mom ran off when I was two or three, and our father was...difficult. Jerusha raised me, for the most part."

"That must have made her death even harder for you to bear," she said softly.

"You could say that."

He pulled his hand away from hers. Even now, twenty-four years later, if he gave rein to his emotions, he would be consumed with rage and fury, all directed at one man.

Silas Davis.

"It was so senseless. Jerusha was a sweet girl, kind and gentle. I wouldn't say she was simple but she had a gentle spirit. She just looked at the world and tried to see the good in everyone, no matter how despicable they were."

She used to hold him after the rantings and the beatings and tell him their father wasn't a bad man, that he was hurting and mad and missed their mama.

Cale had known, even at ten, that Silas was pure evil.

He let out a breath, hating this part and wondering why telling it never seemed to get easier. "When she was thirteen, my father gave her into marriage to a fellow elder in his fundamentalist church. He was fifty-six and Jerusha was his fourth wife. She endured six months of it before she escaped by swallowing a bottle of painkillers."

Jerusha might have taken her life, but Cale had never blamed her. He knew exactly who was responsible. Silas killed his own daughter just as surely as if he'd forced the pills down her throat.

He had never experienced such all-consuming grief and rage as he had the day he had heard of his sister's suicide. Silas hadn't even deigned to tell him, as if it were some pesky little detail he couldn't be bothered about.

Cale had to hear the whispers at the Sunday service he was always forced to attend, had to endure the sidelong looks, until finally the murmurs grew loud enough for him to hear and finally to understand.

When he realized what had happened, he had wanted to puke, to scream and rage and howl.

All their lives, Jerusha had tried to stand between Caleb and their father. They had both endured Silas's wrath, his frequent diatribes about how they were both destined for the fires of hell. They were spawns of Satan, Silas was fond of reminding both of them, because their mother had been a whore and a jezebel.

Caleb seemed to inspire more of his father's wrath. He was never sure exactly why, maybe because he looked more like the slender, dark-haired mother he vaguely remembered, or maybe just because he was the younger and weaker of the two siblings.

Jerusha did her best to deflect Silas's attention. She had tried to distract him, or failing that, she had turned his wrath toward her and taken the beating meant for him.

When she couldn't—or didn't dare, for fear of making things worse—she had comforted him and tended to the blisters on his back and legs.

She had been his protector, his confidante and his best friend. Yet he had been completely helpless to protect her, just a twelve-year-old boy, while she was victimized over and over again.

Knowing he had failed to help her escape, that she had chosen to take the only way out available to her, had sparked a primal, visceral rage inside him.

He hadn't taken time to think it through, had reacted completely out of raw emotion. He had reached into his pocket of his scratchy wool Sunday pants that were already three inches too short for him and his fingers encountered cold metal, the pocketknife Jerusha had given him for his twelfth birthday.

With a wild, frantic bloodlust, he had gone after the bastard who had sired him. He would have gone for his throat if he could have reached it. Instead, he had struck blindly, over and over.

He had no doubt he would have killed his father if he'd had the chance. God surely knew how much he'd wanted to.

He didn't realize his hand had curled into a fist now until Megan covered it again with her own fingers, cool and small and soft.

His throat ached. In that instant, something hard and tight in his chest—something that seemed to have expanded since that horrible day two weeks earlier, until he could barely breathe around it—seemed to shake loose.

For several long moments, he could only focus on taking one breath and then another, shocked to his core at how close he was to the breaking point. This was insane.

What the hell was he doing, burdening her with this when she was living through every parent's worst nightmare? He should stop right now, run as fast and far away from Megan Vance as he could.

He rose, desperate for distance between them. "You don't want to hear all this."

"What did you do?" she asked quietly, ignoring his statement.

He had come this far, he might as well tell her the rest of it. He sighed and sat back down.

"You could say I didn't take the news well. I attacked my father with a pocketknife and stabbed him several times before others in the congregation pulled me off."

Megan digested his matter-of-fact words, her mind caught on the stark image of a skinny, dark-haired boy acting out of rage and pain. She probably should have been shocked by his words but all she could manage was a deep satisfaction.

"Good," she said. "Any father who would do such a hideous thing to his own daughter deserves no less."

Cale blinked in surprise at her words and she thought she saw some of the shadows in his eyes lift a little.

"I didn't do much damage," he said. "It was only a pocketknife, and not a very sharp one at that."

"What happened to you?"

What had turned that grieving boy into the hardened man sitting beside her? she wondered. She was genuinely interested, she realized, and even grateful for the temporary distraction from her all-consuming fear over Cameron.

There was an odd intimacy to sitting beside him in her quiet house after midnight while most of the world slept. Out of habit, she reached for her knitting bag from the table next to the couch and put her hands to work as she waited for him to decide if he wanted to share any more pieces of his life with her.

"I spent a year in juvenile detention. Would have been longer except the family court judge considered the extenuating circumstances. I think by the time my father had finished his diatribe against the evils of our flawed system of justice and the heretics who dared to pass judgment in God's stead, the judge would have liked to take a pocketknife to him, as well."

She couldn't begin to imagine such an upbringing. She thought of her own father, how patient and attentive he had been through her mother's long illness, how he had worked so hard to provide for his family.

Even though he was a tough Boston cop, Paul Kincaid had been a gentle, kind man at home, always willing to pull his daughter onto his lap for a story or spend time in the backyard with Kevin throwing baseballs.

"You didn't go back home after your release, did you?"

His laugh was harsh and abrupt. She yearned to touch him in comfort again, but she hadn't missed the way he had pulled away when she had tried before.

She sensed he wasn't a man easy with softness and compassion. She also sensed he didn't offer the details of his past to many people, and she couldn't help feeling a little honored that he seemed willing to share them with her now.

"The court system decided that probably wasn't such a great idea, especially after I told the judge I would stab him all over again if I ever had to spend another minute in his company. Silas wouldn't have taken me back anyway. I was as dead to him as Jerusha. Breaking the fifth commandment, you know. The one about honoring your father, even when he's a zealous, self-righteous son of a bitch."

Through the cotton of the FBI T-shirt, he rubbed his shoulder absently, a gesture she suspected was completely unconscious. She wondered again if he was the injured agent Molly had heard about on the news but didn't know how to ask.

"No, I didn't go back," he said after a moment. "I was put into foster care and bounced around between group homes until I went to college a few years later."

Surviving such a troubled adolescence must have had a profound impact on his life and the choices he made since.

"Is what happened to your sister the reason you turned to law enforcement?" she asked. "Why you work to protect children?"

He stiffened beside her and she immediately regretted the personal question. "I'm sorry. Forget I asked that."

"No. It's, uh, just not something I spend much time thinking about. I suppose you're right. After Quantico, I gravitated directly to the CAC unit—Crimes Against Children—though it's not an assignment many agents actively seek."

"It can't always be an easy line of work."

Something dark and almost tortured flickered in his gaze before he looked away. "Not always, no."

She sensed he wanted to say more, but he let his words linger between them. He must see horrible things, things she couldn't even conceive of. She knew the depth of her own fear and uncertainty over her son. How could he walk in the midst of this pain all the time?

She imagined it would be immensely satisfying to put child predators behind bars but the process of investigating them and gathering evidence must be both unhealthy and heartbreaking.

She wanted to ask him how he coped with it, what kind of survival methods he used to separate himself from all that emotion. But she before she could find the words, she heard the thud of boots on the porch and a moment later, Daniel Galvez walked into the great room.

If the sheriff considered it odd to find her sitting in a dimly lit room with the FBI agent, her knitting in her lap and a scrapbook open on the table before them, he didn't indicate it by any alteration of expression. His handsome features remained as hard and remote as ever.

He looked tired, she thought, and she was once more filled with an overwhelming gratitude for all the men and women who had put their lives on hold to look for her son.

"Megan, you shouldn't be here all night. What can I say to convince you to go on back to Scott and Molly's place to sleep for a few hours?"

"Nothing. I need to be here."

"You're a stubborn woman."

She shook her head. "I'm just a mother."

His smile looked ragged around the edges. "Which makes you about the most formidable creature on earth, in my book."

He turned to the FBI agent. "I'm gathering the incident team for an update and a strategy session in about fifteen minutes out in the command center if you're interested."

"I'll be there."

Megan desperately wanted to go, but she knew she wouldn't be welcome.

"I'll see you in a few minutes," Daniel said, then walked out of the house again, leaving a sudden awkward silence in his wake.

For some strange reason, after the sheriff left, she found herself keenly aware that she and Cale were alone in the house, something that hadn't truly registered before. The sheriff's presence had somehow put an end to any shared confidences.

Cale seemed to sense it to. He rose. "I should go."

"Right."

She didn't want him to go, she realized with some surprise. She wouldn't have expected it and she didn't quite understand it, but when she was with him, she somehow didn't feel so afraid.

"I hate to play the same old song here since I'm pretty fond of my eyeballs, but you need to get some rest," he said. "You're not going to be any good to Cameron or to your daughter if you wear yourself to the bone. It would be better if you went to your sister's house for a few hours. Will you at least think about it?"

"I'll think about it." She just wouldn't *do* it, but she wasn't about to tell him that. "Agent Davis…"

He turned at the door. "Yes?"

"I know my presence is not really welcome at these briefings. I accept that. Sheriff Galvez made it clear earlier, as gently as possible, that the information in the briefings is raw and unfiltered, and many leads will turn out to be erroneous. I understand that. I do. But this is my son. Please. I need to know what's happening. Could you…could you keep me as informed as possible? I hate not knowing what's going on. I know it's probably not…not strictly procedure. But I need to know."

A muscle tightened his jaw. "I'll tell you what I can, Megan," he said after a moment. "That's all I can promise."

She mustered a shaky smile. "Thank you."

He gazed at her for a moment, then shook his head. "Get some rest," he urged again, his voice gruff, before he walked outside.

Chapter 8

7:00 a.m., Day Two

Nobody would ever know what happened to him.

Cameron lay on his side in the dark, his arms curled up around his drawn-up knees and fought down terrified, lonely tears. His mom would be going crazy with worry by now and he felt terrible about it.

He was so stupid. He should never have come in here. It had all been a dumb game, just a stupid game. How had everything turned out to be so awful?

He was so thirsty. He had finished the last of his water a couple hours ago, and he hadn't eaten since the night before.

He would give just about anything right now for a big bowl of Froot Loops and milk, and a giant glass of ice-cold orange juice to go with it.

Cameron sniffled a little and made himself sit up, even though he was so tired, more tired than the time he got to have his best friend Jason sleep over back in San Diego before they moved. They stayed up until way late, playing Nintendo and watching DVDs, and had an awesome time, but the next day he had been so tired he just lay around all day.

He had tried to sleep in the night but he wasn't sure how much rest he'd had. He had been too uncomfortable lying on the ground, and he hated the dark.

He was tired and cold. If that wasn't enough, he had a weird, jittery feeling in his stomach, and his head was pounding like a whole cave full of rocks had fallen on it.

Was this his second day since he snuck out of his room and saw the shooting? Or was it the third? He couldn't seem to keep track of time.

He cried out suddenly when he heard another rumble somewhere in the cave and the clatter of rocks. He was so scared and didn't know what to do. He had used up the last flashlight batteries an hour ago and now all he had was the face of his watch, and that was getting dimmer and dimmer all the time.

He didn't dare move without a light, not after he fell down that shaft. All he could do was curl up here with the darkness pressing in on him.

Was this what it was like in a coffin?

He whimpered at that image. He didn't want to die. But at least he would be with his dad now. Cam was scared about dying, but he found some comfort that he would at least have his dad around in heaven to show him around and stuff.

He was sure going to miss his mom and Hailey,

though. He wiped the tears trickling down his cheek with his grimy T-shirt.

"I'm sorry, Mommy," he whispered, wishing with all his heart she could somehow hear him. "I'm really sorry. I was wrong to sneak out. Don't be too sad, okay?"

He rolled over, wishing this pounding in his head would just stop.

This was hell. Worse than hell. It was the deepest, darkest, most terrible purgatory any parent should have to endure.

Megan sat dry-eyed at the kitchen table, her millionth cup of lousy coffee cooling in her hands. She had been awake for about thirty hours now, except for the few minutes she had drifted off out of sheer exhaustion.

She had awakened a half hour or so later to find someone had covered her with one of the legion of afghans she had knitted in the long hours of the night during those horrible days after Rick's death.

She wasn't sure who it was who had covered her, but she suspected the man sitting across from her at the kitchen table.

"Are you sure nothing has changed?" she asked Agent Davis, as if repeating the same question a dozen times might change his answer.

"The search in the mountains is expanding, with more volunteer searchers expected to show up today."

He made a face at the terrible coffee and set it away from him. He looked alert and competent, though she knew he hadn't slept any more than she. He couldn't have, since he had spent much of the night in the house with her, except for the occasional briefings with Sheriff Galvez.

She had no idea how he pulled off seeming so composed when she felt as if she had been dragged behind a tractor for two or three days, but she was grateful for it.

Though she didn't understand exactly why, somehow she felt a little better whenever she was with Agent Davis. The world seemed a little brighter, a little more hopeful.

He wouldn't rest until her son was found. She knew it with complete certainty, especially after learning the bits of his past he had shared with her the night before.

"The hotline is still flooded with tips," he went on. "But I'm afraid not many of them are going anywhere. It's a new day, though. Anything can happen."

She didn't necessarily consider that a good thing. "I know I don't have to tell you the urgency. Cameron has now missed three doses of his seizure meds. If we don't find him soon, there's a real risk of him going into a prolonged epileptic state. *Status epilepticus.*"

"I'm assuming by the sound of that, it's a bad thing."

"Terrible! It can cause respiratory distress, sustained loss of consciousness. Even death."

His mouth tightened and she saw her own frustration reflected in the polar blue of his eyes. "We're missing something. I can feel it. I just don't know where else to go."

He sighed. "Gage should be here in a few minutes. Maybe he'll have a fresh take on things."

The back door opened before she could answer and a little red-haired dynamo burst through. Megan's spirits lifted at the sight of her daughter, her hair in fresh braids and her doll tucked tight under her arm.

Hailey rushed to her and Megan held her close, feeling some of the tightness around her heart ease.

"Hi, Mommy!" Hailey chirped. "We brought you breakfast. Aunt Molly said you would forget to eat, so we made you muffins. They're chocolate chip and banana. I had three already and they are *good*."

"They sound good. I'll have one in a minute, honey." For now, she only wanted to sit here and hold her child.

"It's a madhouse out between your house and ours," Molly exclaimed. "I thought we had a lot of media interest yesterday, but now you can't even move through the media vans and mobile uplink units out there."

The story had hit the national news with a vengeance the night before. She could only pray the extra media attention would help and not hinder the search.

"Hi, Caleb Davis." Hailey smiled across the table at the FBI agent.

Megan met his gaze and saw the same strained look in his eyes she had seen the day before when he had first seen her daughter. Was it something about Hailey? she wondered.

"Morning," he said somewhat tersely. He rose to leave, but Hailey stopped him by slipping away from her mother and thrusting the basket of muffins at him.

"You can have a muffin if you want. Me and Aunt Molly made them for my mom, but you should eat one too, so you won't go hungry while you look for Cameron."

He just couldn't figure out a graceful way to refuse this sweet little girl with her missing teeth and her braids. He finally reached into the basket and pulled one out. His shoulder suddenly throbbed and he didn't think it was a coincidence.

Hailey didn't really look anything like Soshi Decker, except for the missing teeth. But when he saw her fresh-faced innocence, his brain kept flashing to images of Soshi gurgling and gasping and trying to stay alive as her blood flowed to the wooden floor of that damn cabin.

"Uh, thanks," he said, pushing those grim images as far away as he could.

He needed to leave this warm, sunlit kitchen. He needed to go out and do something physical. Maybe he would ask Daniel if he could take a turn searching the backcountry. McKinnon wouldn't like it, but he was fairly sure his partner would understand.

"It's good, isn't it?" Hailey asked him with an eager smile.

He chewed and swallowed a mouthful of fragrant muffin. He imagined it probably tasted delicious but when he was focused on a case like this, everything seemed to taste the same.

"It's great," he managed to say with enough conviction he was fairly sure could convince a six-year-old. He looked at her smile, so much like her mother's, then set the muffin down abruptly as a stunning thought occurred to him.

How the hell could he have missed such an obvious source of information? In all this craziness, had anybody bothered to ask Hailey about her brother's whereabouts?

Megan and her sister were busy discussing a strategy for the media statements Molly, as the family spokesperson, would be making throughout the day.

He took advantage of their distraction to pull Hailey slightly away from them, using the excuse that he needed help finding a glass for some water to go with the muffin.

She helped him eagerly and after he filled the glass with water and they stood at the sink, he considered the best way to approach her. He wasn't sure he was in the best place mentally to interrogate a six-year-old girl right now, but Gage wasn't here yet and he was suddenly filled with an urgency he couldn't explain.

"You know there are a lot of people out there looking for your brother," he finally began.

She nodded, solemn suddenly at the reminder of Cameron. "I know they are. I prayed really hard that they would find him today and he could come home. Do you think he will?"

"I hope so, sweetheart."

He crouched down to her level. "Hailey, I want you to think about something and think about it really hard, okay?"

"Okay." She looked confused and a little nervous, and he hoped to hell he wasn't blowing this.

"If you were the boss of all those people who are out there looking for Cameron, is there any place you would tell them to look? Any place at all where you think he might go?"

"Like where?"

"I don't know. Does Cameron have a special place? Did he ever talk to you about any place he would like to go?"

Her brow furrowed as she considered his words. "I don't know," she said after a moment. "Maybe the big hole."

His heart seemed to stutter in his chest, and he was fairly certain he would have toppled over if not for the kitchen cupboard holding him up. "What big hole, Hailey?" he managed through a throat suddenly dry.

She pressed a hand over her mouth as if to yank the words back. "I'm not supposed to say. Cam will be mad."

"What aren't you supposed to say?"

She looked around to see if anyone else had overheard them. He followed her gaze and saw Molly and Megan were still busy at the table. "It's Cam's secret place," she whispered. "He said if I told, he would cut off all my hair in the middle of the night. I don't want to be bald."

Cale drew in a ragged breath. "Sweetheart, your brother might be hurt somewhere. I promise, he's not going to be mad at you for telling. He would *want* you to tell me so we can find him and bring him home to have one of these yummy muffins."

She held the basket out to him again, momentarily distracted. "I helped Aunt Molly add the chocolate chips. I even got to work the mixer thing. But I can't lick the spoon because that can make you sick."

"Right. You worked really hard to make these muffins, and I know you would want your brother to come home so he can have one. If he is in the big hole like you said, we need to help him so he can get out of there and come home."

"And my mommy and Aunt Molly and everybody won't be so sad?" she asked.

"I promise." He only hoped it was a vow he could keep. "Tell me about the big hole Cameron found."

Hailey scratched her chin and studied him for a minute. He had never been so grateful for anything in his life when she seemed to reach a decision to trust him.

"One time we were supposed to stay in the yard but Cameron wanted to go 'sploring, so we snuck under the fence and went to look for rabbits on the mountain. We saw one go behind a rock and we followed it and found the hole. We looked in but we didn't have a flashlight."

"It was a cave?"

"I guess. Cam wanted to go in, but I said I was gonna tell and he called me a big tattletale."

She cast a furtive look at her mother, then looked back at him. "We went home," she said, her voice low. "But I think Cameron went back a different day."

He flashed back to the photographs he and Megan had looked at the evening before of Cameron caving Timpanogas with his father, of the bright enthusiasm on the boy's face.

The kid had, by all accounts, used tiny finger holes to climb out of his two-story bedroom window.

It wasn't a stretch at all to imagine him wanting to explore the murky delights of a cave on his own.

"Why do you say that?" he asked Hailey.

"One time he left with his backpack and wouldn't let me go with him. He said I was a stupid girl and would be too slow. He said if I told Mommy, he would cut off all my hair *and* he would hide my Holly Hobbie somewhere I would never find her."

Adrenaline gushed over him, and it was all he could do not to reach out and kiss Hailey right in the middle of her little forehead. This was it, the lead they had been looking for. He knew it, with a gut-deep assurance he couldn't explain.

"Do you remember how to get to the big hole?" he asked.

She cocked her head, frowning with concentration. "I don't know. Probably. All the rocks kind of look the same, but I think I remember how to find it. It's shaped like a boat, kind of."

"Is it a long way from here?"

She shrugged. "Kind of. I don't know if you can go. You have to crawl under a fence and you might be too big."

"Maybe I can climb over it."

"That might work."

He rose, eager to go, even as prudence warned him to handle this carefully. He couldn't just haul Hailey up on the mountainside without explaining to her mother what was happening, but he hated the idea of raising false hope in Megan if the lead didn't go anywhere.

"I'm going to talk to your mom for a minute, and then you and I will go see if we can find the big hole, okay?"

"And Cameron?"

"I hope so, sweetheart. I really hope so."

He approached the table, considering his words carefully even as his heart pumped with excitement. A hidden cave. That could explain why they hadn't found any trace of him.

As encouraging as he found the information, he knew they were a long way from having the boy home safe. If the boy had found some kind of cave and tried to explore it on his own, Cale knew from his own caving experience that a hundred different hazards awaited a lone nine-year-old boy inside, anything from cave-ins to hazardous gases to hypothermia.

"Megan, I need to borrow Hailey for a few moments."

She frowned in confusion. "Hailey? Whatever for?"

He let out a breath and plunged forward. "She has a possible lead into where Cameron might have gone."

She and her sister stared at him, their similar green eyes dark with shock. "What?! Where?" Megan exclaimed.

He was uncomfortably aware of her sister looking on but couldn't keep himself from reaching for Megan's hand. "Look, I don't want you to get your hopes up, but Hailey said she and Cameron stumbled onto some kind of cave or something up in the foothills one day when they were playing. They didn't go inside that time, but she seems to think there's a chance he might have gone back to explore it later."

A bright and terrible hope flared in her eyes, warring with disbelief. "He wouldn't!"

"I'm not so sure of that, from what you've told me about him and what evidence I've seen myself."

Her fingers fluttered in his. "Oh, dear heavens. Anything could have happened to him in there!"

"Calm down, Megan. I know it's hard, but let's not get ahead of ourselves. Hailey is only six years old. We have to keep in mind that her information might not be the most reliable."

She bristled, a mother bear defending her cub. "She's very smart for her age."

"I can tell that. But she also knows how much everyone wants to find Cameron. How much *she* wants to find him. She might be letting her own imagination run wild on her."

"But you don't think so."

He squeezed her fingers. "At this point I don't know. But I promised you I would keep you as informed as possible, so that's why I'm telling you. If it's all right with you, I'd like to take Hailey up and see if she can find the spot again."

"Of course. I'm coming with you."

He wanted to argue with her, but he had seen that stubborn light in her eyes enough over the course of the last twenty-four hours to know it would be useless.

Besides, Hailey was her daughter. She had the right to accompany her, whether he liked it or not.

"Even if Hailey can find the cave opening again, you have to understand that we can't go inside without proper gear and trained personnel," he warned. "It's too dangerous."

"Of course. Let's go."

"Wait here. I need to brief the sheriff on this new information."

"Hurry," she urged, and he hoped to hell he wasn't setting her up for another crushing disappointment.

She knew Cale's advice not to pin all her hopes on this possibility was wise. But as she and Sheriff Galvez followed him and Hailey through thick sagebrush and scrub oak, Megan couldn't help the flutters of anticipation in her chest.

Cameron was close. She could feel it. They had to be on the right track. They *had* to be.

After the men helped her and Hailey over the wire fence between her property and the Forest Service land bordering it, they walked steadily uphill. Her house was in sight the entire time, and from here she could see the bustle of activity from the media and the searchers coming and going.

The morning was cool and lovely, in sharp contrast to the hot wind of the day before. The air was sweet with the scent of sage and rubber rabbit brush and mule ear daisies, familiar smells she had come to love in her few months here.

She had walked this deer trail often with her children, and they usually surprised a rabbit or deer or the occasional elk. One evening, they had even seen a lone coyote on the ridgeline, though he had loped away the moment he caught their scent.

"Are we getting closer?" Cale asked Hailey when they had climbed perhaps a quarter mile from the house.

"Yeah," Hailey said. She pointed to a stand of scrub oak ahead of them. "On the other side of those little trees."

Doubt started to creep in again as Megan registered their location. "I've walked that way many times before and never noticed any kind of cave," she said to Daniel.

She had to believe Hailey's story, though. Her daughter surely wouldn't make up a fib about something so important.

"There are old abandoned mines all over this area," the sheriff answered. "The federal government made a big push several years ago to seal off all the entrances and bulldoze over them to keep people from wandering in and being hurt."

She let out a breath as a host of grim possibilities flashed through her mind. "Is it possible one slipped through the cracks?"

"Who knows? I've got investigators checking with the Bureau of Land Management and the Forest Service to see what kind of history there might be here and if they can track any caves or mines."

The location had been a huge selling point when she had been house-hunting. She had immediately fallen in love with the house. Besides its charm and proximity to Scott and Molly, she had loved the idea of having no neighbors behind her and being able to enjoy such wildness out her kitchen window.

Now she was cursing the day she had even seen the place.

"This is quite a long way from the house," she said. "Could he have made it by himself in the dark?"

"He probably viewed it as a big adventure," Daniel answered.

"There." From in front of them, Hailey suddenly pointed to a jagged pile of rocks.

"Are you sure?" Cale asked her.

Hailey nodded. "I remember. See? It looks like a big sailboat."

They moved closer, and Megan was afraid her heart would pound out of her chest.

If Hailey hadn't pointed it out for them, Megan knew the searchers scouring these mountains never would have found this spot on their own.

"I know this is the right rock," Hailey said with a frown. "But all those bushes weren't there before."

The sheriff grabbed the pile of brush and started to pull it aside. "Someone has deliberately concealed the opening."

When he and Cale finished clearing away the brush, they revealed an opening between two of the rocks, perhaps three feet square.

"I told you it was a big hole," Hailey said.

Megan hugged her daughter, unable to breathe for her growing excitement. Cameron was in there. She could feel it.

"You were right, sweetheart. You were absolutely right."

Chapter 9

"You and Hailey wait here," Cale said. "We're just going to go inside a little, to see if we can find any evidence Cameron might have been here and to figure out what we might be up against."

She wanted to protest—she couldn't bear any more of this endless waiting, and she wanted to run into that blackness herself to find her son. But she knew the cave was no place for her daughter. Instead, she nodded, pulling Hailey onto her lap.

She passed the time while they waited by telling Hailey how proud she was of her remembering the cave and talking to her about what she was most looking forward to when she started first grade at her new school in only a few weeks.

After what felt like eons—but was probably no more than five or six minutes—the men returned.

Their excitement was palpable. She could sense it the moment they emerged into the sunlight.

She rose and set Hailey down, holding her hand tight. "What is it? What did you find?"

The sheriff held out a small black jacket. "That's Cameron's!" she exclaimed. The blood drained from her head and her vision wobbled, sending the slit in the mountains wavering in front of her eyes.

She swayed a little, a combination of exhaustion and stress, but before she could gather the strength to steady herself, Cale hurried forward and caught her in his strong arms.

How had she come to rely on him in such a short time? she wondered. How had he become so important, this lean but powerful pillar of strength through this terrible time?

"Stay with me, Meg. Come on."

She drew in a breath, gathering her control, then stepped away from him. "I'm sorry. I'm sorry. I'm fine. That's Cameron's jacket. I bought it for him last month for school."

"When was the last time you saw it?"

"I don't know. Right after I bought it, I suppose. He took all his new school clothes to his room."

"That doesn't mean he's down there," he warned her. "It only means he's been inside at some point in the last month."

"He's there, Cale. I know it."

She hugged him tightly, unable to contain the emotions pouring through her. He returned the embrace for a moment, then set her away from him. "You're going to have to be patient, Megan. I know it will be tough after you've already waited so long, but moving the search underground will be a long, tedious process. We're going to have to bring in searchers trained in this kind of rescue, and that's going to take some time."

"Why can't we go inside and look now?"

"An underground rescue is one of the most dangerous operations for searchers. We don't know what we're facing in there, what kind of conditions we'll find, so we have to be prepared for anything. It's going to take time and I think you need to go back to the house. Daniel is calling for an all-terrain vehicle to take you two down the mountain."

She hated to come so close to her son only to retreat again. "I'm fine here."

He squeezed her hand. "I think you're both better off waiting down at the house. Especially Hailey. We don't know how long this is going to take or what we're going to find, Megan."

She drew in a shuddering breath at the grim reminder. Finding the jacket might be an encouraging sign but the search was far from over—and there was no guarantee it would end happily.

Cameron had been missing for more than thirty hours and she couldn't bear thinking of all the things that could have happened to him in that time, especially if he *had* ventured into this underground deathtrap.

"All right," she said after a moment. "We'll go back down the mountain and wait."

"I'll keep you informed on how things are going, Megan. I swear it. I've got both climbing and caving experience, so I will be there every step of the way."

A wave of warmth washed over her for this man

who had been a stranger only the day before. "I can never thank you enough for all you've done. I don't know if I would have made it through the night without you."

He looked uncomfortable at her words but was spared from having to answer by the arrival of a small off-road vehicle driven by one of the sheriff's deputies.

"You can thank me after we find him safe and sound."

She wanted desperately to believe she would have that chance. With one last shaky smile, she gathered Hailey and climbed into the off-road vehicle.

"No way in hell. You're not going in there."

Cale barely spared his partner a look as he continued cinching on his harness. "How are you planning to stop me?"

"I've got Flex-Cufs or regular handcuffs. Take your pick."

"Sorry, partner, but I'm choosing door number three."

They stood in front of the mine entrance where he and Daniel had managed to round up some improvised cave gear that would at least let them get started while they waited for reinforcements.

The county's only two volunteer firefighters trained in underground rescue had been searching all night for Cameron and had been sent home a few hours earlier. They had been called back but wouldn't be there for a while. Other counties in the state were sending reinforcements, but in the meantime, he and Daniel had decided to take a cursory look around until they could arrive.

Cale couldn't have explained his urgency but something told him they needed to get the search going right away. Cameron needed his seizure medication as soon as possible. Even an hour's delay seemed too long.

Gage didn't seem to feel the same urgency Cale did. His partner frowned at him. "You're two weeks off a gunshot wound. You know you're in no physical shape for an underground rescue."

"I'm fine. You can stop babysitting me now, Gage."

"This is so far against regulation it's not even in the same stratosphere of the agency rule book. You're an FBI agent, not some Rescue Ranger. Curtis is going to have both our asses for this."

"Our assignment was to help find Cameron Vance. That's exactly what I'm doing."

His partner opened his mouth to argue but Cale cut him off. "Gage, I know what I'm doing. There are only two people here right now who have ever participated in a cave rescue before. One of them is Daniel Galvez, and I'm the other one. This is my decision. We can't afford to waste time waiting for other trained personnel to arrive from other parts of the state, not when the sheriff and I can go in now."

"You've been up all night and your arm is nowhere near healed. How much help do you really think you're going to be?"

He had considered both of those facts. But he knew he had no choice. "I need to do this."

His partner studied him for a long moment, then sighed and backed down. Cale wondered at the reason for it. Could McKinnon see the desperate hope in his eyes, the urgency burning inside him to do everything he could to expedite a happy ending in this case?

It didn't make any sense, he knew, but somehow

finding Cameron Vance had become vital to healing the jagged, gaping wounds on his soul from the events of two weeks earlier.

"Be careful," McKinnon said.

Cale managed a smile as the sheriff approached them. "I'm always careful."

"Ready?" Galvez asked.

"Let's do it."

Inside the dark chamber, the air was cool, heavy, pressing in on all sides. Their helmet lights played off earthen and rock walls shored up by rotting timbers. He couldn't begin to guess how old this mine was. The possibility for cave-ins was a real danger.

They moved into the mine with Daniel in the lead. The tunnel was a straight shot and pretty easygoing at first. He could definitely see how this would appeal to a young boy.

They sloped slightly downhill for about twenty feet before they hit their first intersection. In a typical cave rescue with various teams, they would split here and explore both directions until they found some evidence of the missing caver.

Since they didn't have that luxury, Cale figured they would have to roll the dice, until his headlamp picked up an unmistakable clue.

"See that?" Daniel asked.

Cale traced the white chalk arrow, low on the earthen wall. "This kid is no dummy."

"Let's hope he's smart enough to stay alive in here," the sheriff replied grimly.

"I've got a feeling we're not going to have arrows showing us the whole way, but let's start in that direction. Do you agree?"

Daniel nodded and Cale took the lead. Both men had to crouch at various points along the mine shaft. They encountered two forks in about fifty yards, leading in opposite directions. Each time, they found another chalk arrow pointing them in the direction they needed to go.

At the second fork, the shaft suddenly angled steeply upward and Cale was suddenly aware of an odd smell. Something familiar and sharp, like cat urine.

"Smell that?" he asked Daniel, instinctively yanking up his mask with one hand and pulling out his weapon with the other.

The sheriff nodded, yanking up a mask, as well. "I know that smell." The mask muffled his voice and he spoke low, pulling out his own sidearm. "I've busted four meth labs around here in the last six months."

"Who's stupid enough to cook in a damn cave?" Cale whispered.

"You wouldn't believe the places where they can set up an operation. We've got a real problem in the middle of the wilderness. Hikers have stumbled onto several meth labs."

Both of them shut off their headlamps and were immediately pitched into blackness. No trace of light appeared, which was a hopeful sign that this was an old cook site and no one was around.

Still, the sheriff turned on a small flashlight that only provided focused light and eased up the incline carefully. Cale let him take over point. This was his territory, his county. He was just along for the ride.

All kinds of grim scenarios ran through his brain as he inched up behind the sheriff. A curious nine-year-old boy and a meth cook were not a combination that boded well for a good outcome, and he hated considering the possibilities.

At the top of the incline, the sheriff made room for him beside him and Cale realized they were looking down on a large chamber, perhaps twenty feet in circumference.

The sheriff took a chance and turned on his head-lamp, illuminating the space below. It was obvious this was a cold site, though they found plenty of evidence it had been used as a lab. There were empty bottles of chemicals, tubing, beakers, a camp stove. Everything necessary for a large-scale meth lab.

They climbed down into the chamber. "You think Cameron Vance stumbled on to this?" Cale voiced his fear aloud.

"I surely hope not."

He moved around the chamber, looking for some clue the boy might have been here. Another tunnel led off from the main chamber. To the left of it, Cale spied a vertical shaft. He aimed his headlamp down and felt all the air leave his lungs.

"Dan! Bring your light over here!"

The sheriff hurried over and aimed his headlamp into the abyss. The combined force of their lights played off a body crumpled at an awkward angle, the features gray and motionless.

Cale wasn't even aware of the long string of bitter curses spewing out of him until Daniel laid a hand on his arm.

"It's not the boy, Cale. I know this guy. We've just found our missing pothead. And by the looks of those rubber gloves on his hands, I would guess Wally Simon branched out into meth cooking, too."

He took a ragged breath, pushing away the cold despair that had washed over him at the first sight of that body. He had lost any trace of objectivity and distance in this case, he realized grimly.

"You think he was tweaking and fell?" he asked.

"Maybe. I would guess though that the bullet hole in his forehead had something to do with his death."

Cale sighed, grateful the sheriff was a good enough friend he would probably be willing to overlook his stupidity.

Definitely a bullet hole, he saw now as he looked closer. Had Cameron Vance stumbled onto a drug-related murder? If so, were they going to find his bullet-riddled body dumped somewhere in here?

His stomach burned at the possibility and he knew if they did, he would have to quit the job. He couldn't do this anymore, not if he had to be the one to tell Megan her son was dead.

"I have to call this in, Cale," Daniel said, reaching for the World War II-era military field telephone they had rounded up, since modern cell phones and radio receivers wouldn't work underground.

"Wait. You've got to tell Megan first. You know how word spreads on a rescue like this. I don't want her hearing we found a body in here without knowing the full story."

"Yeah, you're right." A moment later, Daniel spoke into the phone to the communications specialist from the search and rescue unit who was standing by on the other end. "Fletcher, this is Galvez. I need you to patch me to Mrs. Vance's cell phone."

He handed the phone to Cale. "You tell her. You have a better rapport with her than I do."

Before Cale could protest that he had no such thing, Megan answered, a half hopeful, half terrified note in her voice as she said hello.

"Megan—" he began, but she cut him off before he could say more.

"Have you found him?"

"No. Listen to me. We have *not* found him. We found a body inside the mine, but it is not Cameron. Repeat, it is *not* Cameron. Do you understand me?"

There was a long silence on the other end. "A…a body? Whose body?" Her voice sounded baffled and frightened and he wanted more than anything to be with her to pull her into his arms.

"I can't say anything about that yet. But I *can* tell you with a hundred percent certainty it is not your son. We're going to keep looking for Cameron, but I didn't want you to hear the radio chatter about us finding a dead body in here and reach the wrong conclusion, okay?"

"You're sure it's not him?"

"Absolutely."

"All right." She still sounded wary, but the abject fear was gone from her voice. "Caleb, be careful."

The tenderness settling in his chest at the concern he heard in her voice terrified him more than anything he was likely to encounter in the mine shafts.

"Right. I'll keep you posted."

He handed the phone back to Daniel, who immediately called the communications specialist again so he could report their discovery.

He knew the sheriff would be busy for some time dealing with the logistics of running an investigation into both a meth lab and a murder, but he was impatient to keep looking.

"I'm going to check a few things out while you're waiting for the reinforcements to work the murder scene. I won't go far."

Daniel nodded, obviously distracted as he listened to whoever was on the other end of the phone. Cale took off down the horizontal shaft that branched off the main chamber.

He hadn't gone far before he spotted the proverbial light at the end of the tunnel, a small glow. He followed it and a few moments later was surprised to emerge on what he deduced was the other side of the slope, quite a bit lower in elevation from where he and Daniel had entered. This entrance was concealed by thick willows and scrub oak, as well, but it was only about twenty feet from a dirt road.

He guessed this had been the entry point for the meth cook. It would be far more convenient and accessible. Why hike a quarter mile uphill to the mine carrying chemicals and cook supplies when you could drive almost right into it?

He returned to the dank mine interior to report his findings to the sheriff. As he backtracked, his mind considered what might have gone on inside the mine.

Had Cameron Vance had the misfortune to wander in and find the drug operation? He didn't know Wally Simon, but he did know meth cooks were a dangerous breed. They were usually users themselves, often tweaking on crank while they mixed and poured deadly chemicals, too hopped up to use any kind of common sense.

Most cooks wouldn't even think about setting up

without a weapon on hand—not just *on* hand, but *in* hand. He couldn't think of too many creatures on earth more deadly than an armed addict crazy enough to shoot battery acid and antifreeze into his bloodstream.

Cameron was a smart kid, though. He took comfort from that. He wanted to be a SEAL like his father. If he could climb out his bedroom window, he had to know enough about stealth tactics that he wouldn't just blunder into a dangerous situation.

Maybe the cook was already dead when Cam found the scene. Or maybe he discovered the drug activity and tried to go for help, but took a wrong turn somewhere.

His gut was telling him the two things were connected—Cam's disappearance and the meth lab they had found. It was entirely too coincidental that Cameron just happened to disappear in the vicinity of a murder scene and illegal drug activity.

He had been gone no longer than ten minutes, but by the time he returned to the main chamber, a half dozen people were milling around, all of them potentially destroying any evidence that Cameron might have been there.

"I'm going to be busy here for a while," Daniel said with an apologetic frown. "But the cavers from Salt Lake County's SAR team are about twenty minutes away."

"I'll keep looking on my own before any trace is completely destroyed," he told the sheriff, who nodded in understanding.

"Keep the phone with you," he said.

Moving quickly, Cale worked his way back in the direction they had come. Several tunnels intersected off this one. One was collapsed, with no room for anything larger than a small dog to make it through. The next one was large enough for him to walk with his head bowed only slightly. He looked around carefully for any sign Cam had been there.

His gaze sharpened on the dirt and debris of the ground. If he wasn't mistaken, that looked like a footprint in the dirt—a small one, too, much too small to be made by anyone but a nine-year-old.

Chapter 10

An hour after Cale had called her to report finding a body inside the mine, Megan sat on her back deck overlooking the foothills, wondering how much more of this endless waiting she could endure with her sanity still intact.

She didn't know what she found more difficult, the waiting or the endless parade of people trying to distract her from it.

She had finally escaped out here for a little solitude after enduring a very difficult half hour with Father Timms, with that sonorous voice of his, who seemed to vacillate between trying as her ecclesiastical leader to help her hang on to some vestige of hope and preparing her for a less-than-desirable outcome.

She hadn't been in Moose Springs long enough to develop any kind of spiritual trust with the man, so she mostly found his presence intrusive and irritating.

He meant well. *Everyone* meant well, she knew. But she honestly didn't think she could bear one more person grabbing her hands and asking her how she was holding up.

No doubt Caleb would probably tell her it wasn't at all healthy to spend so much of this vigil on her own. But when she was alone, she didn't have to worry about anyone else's emotions but her own. She could pour all her energy into praying her son would be returned to her.

Now she sat out here on her favorite rocker, just below her kitchen window, with her knees pulled up, listening to the wind chimes clink and sing softly in a slight breeze that blew down the mountains.

The kitchen window was just above her and through the open window she could hear the faucet go on as someone drew a glass of water.

"You don't have to tell me that, Allie," she heard clearly through the window. It was Cale's partner, Gage McKinnon. She hadn't spoken with him much and had gotten the impression that he was a very competent, if slightly intimidating FBI agent.

She didn't mean to eavesdrop on a private conversation and started to move out of earshot when Cale's name caught her attention.

"I know that," the agent said, a note of frustration in his voice. "Cale is in absolutely no condition to be in those mine tunnels, either physically or emotionally."

She frowned, sliding back into the rocker.

"Don't you think I tried to talk him out of it?" McKinnon said into the phone. "It was like talking to a wall of granite. He had his mind set on it and nothing I said was going to change his mind."

There was quiet for a moment as he listened to the other person on the line. "Yeah. Go ahead and say it, since I know you're dying to. I was wrong to bring him back on this one. As usual, you were right. He said he was ready and I believed him, but obviously he needed more time."

More time for what? Megan wondered. Why was Cale's partner so convinced he shouldn't be searching for Cameron?

"I've never seen him like this," the agent said, and even from out here she could hear the worry in his voice. "He is completely consumed with finding this kid. I've seen him driven on a case before, but never like this."

He paused again, listening to the other party. "Yeah, that's the logical conclusion. This has to do with him feeling like those two little girls died on his watch."

Two little girls? So Cale *was* the FBI agent Molly had heard about. Her heart ached for him, for the sense of failure she knew he must be living with. Heartsick and feeling guilty for eavesdropping, she rose and headed for the back door to go inside, intending to announce her presence before the other agent said anything else.

"I only hope we find the Vance kid safe and sound," the FBI agent said as she opened the door. "I'm afraid any other outcome just might be more than he can handle."

She must have made some noise at that—or maybe he just sensed her presence. The FBI agent whirled to face her, and his mouth tightened. He let out an oath.

"I've got to go, Al. I'll call you later."

He ended the phone call and slipped the phone into his pocket, his hard features tight with regret.

"I'm sorry you heard that. I'm not usually so indiscreet. Only when I'm worrying about a friend."

Cale was her friend, as well. Somehow in the last day he had become someone she cared about, and she wanted to know why his partner was so concerned for his emotional and physical well-being.

"I didn't mean to eavesdrop on your conversation, but I was sitting out on the deck and couldn't help hearing you through the open window. I'm sorry. But, please, can you tell me why you don't think Agent Davis should be in those tunnels looking for my son?"

He closed his eyes for a moment, and she could see reluctance in every line of his body. He didn't want to tell her, she could tell.

"He's not in the best place right now," he finally said slowly. "Cale is still recovering from an injury sustained on the job a few weeks ago and I'm worried he's pushing himself too hard and is going to reinjure his wound."

"You said he's not ready, emotionally or physically. What did you mean?" she pressed. "How was he injured?"

It suddenly seemed vitally important that she know.

The man sighed, his blue eyes dark and murky. After a moment's hesitation, as if he were trying to make up his mind what to say, he leaned against the kitchen sink and spoke.

"Two weeks ago, Cale was shot while trying to find two little girls who had been kidnapped by their father. Andy Decker was mentally ill and had a history of violence toward the girls and their mother, so there was some urgency in trying to find them. We were all running around like crazy, following different leads. Cale discovered Decker had years ago stayed at a remote cabin in the mountains west of the Salt Lake

Valley. It was a slim lead, but he decided to check it out and he walked into a nightmare."

"The man was there?"

"Right. As he approached, he heard gunfire. He identified himself and ordered the shooter to put down his weapon, but Decker was out of control. He came out shooting. Cale took a hit in the shoulder and had no choice but to return fire, only to discover after he had, uh, subdued the suspect that he had tracked Decker down about a minute too late to save either of the girls."

"How old were they?" Her chest ached for him, for the pain and guilt she knew he must live with.

"Six and four." McKinnon cleared his throat. "It wasn't a good scene. The worst was that Cale was completely on his own for far too long. Like I said, this was a remote location and it took about fifteen or twenty minutes after he called it in for help to get there. By the time other officers arrived on the scene, Cale was barely conscious from the loss of blood, but he was still desperately trying to resuscitate both girls. To no avail, I'm afraid."

She tried to catch her cry of distress, but some of it escaped.

Agent McKinnon sighed. "I shouldn't have told you. He won't be happy about it. Cale is one of my closest friends but he's also an intensely private person. He doesn't share pieces of himself very easily."

And yet he had told her about his sister the night before, about his father and his anger and the years he had spent in foster care. She sensed he didn't share that with many people and she wondered again why he had chosen to tell her.

"I'm glad I know."

So many things made a terrible kind of sense now, like the bleak, haunted look in his eyes and the careful way he moved sometimes. He had been shot only a few weeks ago, had survived a terrible ordeal, yet here he was crawling and climbing and squeezing through impossibly tight spaces to find her son.

She pressed trembling fingers to her chest, to the ache spreading there. How could she have ever thought him hard and unfeeling, toughened by his job?

"He assured me over and over he was ready to be back on the job," Agent McKinnon continued. "When I got the call about Cameron and realized the urgency here in finding him, I decided to overlook my own misgivings. There's no other man in the entire agency I would want on board when it comes to finding missing children. But I have to admit, I'm wondering now if he needed another week or two of recovery time. I certainly never expected him to be the point man in an underground rescue effort."

She didn't know what to say, how to ever thank these men for trying to find her son.

She couldn't honestly tell McKinnon she was sorry Caleb had returned to duty in time to work this case. It was completely selfish of her, but she couldn't regret his presence, especially through the long, terrible night. He had sustained her through those dark hours, and she wasn't completely sure she would have made it through without him.

The conditions inside the mine must be full of hazards she couldn't begin to imagine. As an experienced climber and caver, Cale had to have known what he would face. He had gone inside anyway, even with a half-healed gunshot wound. All for a child he had never met.

She was humbled and deeply, deeply moved.

It sucked to feel so close but still so desperately far away.

After two hours underground, Cale knew they were on the right track. They *had* to be. He had found undeniable evidence someone had been this way recently, and he would bet his life it was Cameron. Besides the evidence of more small shoeprints in the dirt, they found a couple of granola bar wrappers, a discarded battery, and occasional chalk marks on the walls that seemed to grow increasingly wobbly.

Working in five two-person teams, the cave rescue units from across the state had spread out throughout the vast labyrinth, each exploring a different shaft to its end point.

Cale knew and liked his partner, Ben Lucero, a paramedic with the Salt Lake County search and rescue unit. They had worked together on some Homeland Security training exercises, and he found the man smart, fast and completely trustworthy on the other end of a rope.

Together they had cleared and marked three tunnels that ended blindly before they found this one that had obvious signs someone had been here recently. This was the most encouraging sign any of the teams had encountered but it was long, exhausting work, especially when he couldn't shake the conviction time was running out.

Now they were at an intersection, trying to look for evidence that would indicate which direction Cameron might have taken.

"I don't see anything obvious. I say we go left," Cale said.

Lucero agreed. "How the hell deep is this mine? We could be here for weeks."

"We won't be. We're close. I can feel it."

"This kid doesn't even have double digits to his age. How did he make it this far on his own?"

"He's a tough little monkey." Cale paused to take a drink from his water bottle, ignoring the pain in his shoulder as he lifted it to his mouth.

Still, he was aware of Lucero watching him carefully. "You doing okay?" the other man asked for about the nine hundredth time.

"Ask me that again and I'm shoving this water bottle down your throat," he growled. "I'm fine."

Lucero laughed, unoffended by his threat. "Just doing my job. I promised McKinnon I'd keep an eye on you in here. Make sure you don't overdo it."

"You girls don't have anything better to talk about?"

"What's more interesting to talk about than an FBI agent throwing his career away while he tries to save the world?"

Not the world. Just one kid.

"I'm not throwing away anything. I'm doing my job."

"I understand you disobeyed a direct order by staying in here."

He sighed. As predicted, the acting special agent in charge hadn't been thrilled to learn about Cale's direct involvement in the search. Curtis had ordered him out immediately. That had been about two hours ago.

"Didn't McKinnon tell you when he was giving you the babysitting instructions? This is off the clock. I'm not acting in an official capacity here, I'm strictly a volunteer searcher."

Lucero laughed. "Good luck with that one. Let me know if your boss buys it."

Cale didn't care about the acting SAC throwing a temper tantrum. He might get a censure on his record but Moyer, his *real* boss, wouldn't let him be fired over this, not with his record and years of service to the Bureau.

What the hell did a censure matter? The only thing he cared about right now was finding Cameron Vance.

The earth suddenly rumbled around them, another hiccup like the ones they'd been experiencing for the last two hours; up ahead about fifteen feet, dirt and rocks tumbled down.

Both of them crouched, covering their heads, until the rumbling stopped.

"Shit. That was close," Lucero exclaimed. "We're all betting our damn lives in here with these rotting timbers."

"Shut up," Cale snapped.

"Come on. You know as well as I do that these abandoned mines are nothing but unstable death traps."

"Shut up," he repeated, more urgently this time.

To his relief, something in his intensity got through to the other man. He drew his mouth closed, and they both listened closely. Cale thought at first he was imagining things. Then, above the sound of rocks and dirt settling, he heard it again.

A tiny moan.

He knew sounds could be deceiving underground, but he thought it was coming from somewhere past the rockfall.

"Cameron?" he called. He waited for a response as his cry echoed through the tunnel, but all he heard was another small moan.

"This way," he said. They both took off fast, climbing through the unstable rock pile and throwing big stones out of the way so they could get through. On the other side, the tunnel widened so they could stand shoulder to shoulder. The combined force of their headlamps picked up a slight movement and a flash of reflected light. Cale heard another moan.

They moved forward, half running. After another five feet, they saw him, a tiny, battered form curled up on the ground under a reflective survival blanket.

He experienced a wild burst of relief and gratitude, so powerful it made him sway.

"Cameron? Hey, bud, we're here to help you."

He and Lucero knelt down, pulling away the blanket, but the relief didn't last long.

"He's seizing." Lucero stated the obvious. The boy's limbs jerked in convulsive movements and his head twitched to one side. His eyes were open, but the pupils barely reacted to the glare of their headlamps.

"Can you stop it?"

"I don't know. I've got Diastat in my bag, but—"

Before Lucero could finish the thought, the shaft rumbled again and more rocks tumbled down in the direction they had come.

Both he and Lucero bent their bodies over Cameron's to protect the convulsing boy.

"We've got to get out now," Cale yelled. "This whole damn tunnel is coming down."

"Right," Lucero said grimly.

More rocks and dirt showered down, and he was afraid they would all be trapped. When the shower of earth stopped, Cale picked up the boy, trying fiercely not to think about the last time he had held a young, fragile life in his hands, and how disastrously that had ended.

"Go on ahead. I'll bring the boy."

"No way. We're a team. I'm not leaving you."

He didn't waste time arguing, he just headed back the way they had come, his shoulder pulling at even so slight a burden. They ran hard as the tunnel continued to shake, just like the child in his arms.

They had just reached the T-bone intersection when the entire tunnel where Cameron had been lying collapsed behind them, sending dust and debris flying in every direction.

Lucero gasped out a choked curse. "Man, that was close. Five more minutes and this place would have been a tomb for all three of us."

"Come on. Let's get out of here."

He had to admit he was grateful to have Lucero leading the way to help through the tight spots and move larger rocks out of his path as they hurried toward a more stable section of the mine.

"I think we're okay to stop here," Cale finally said. It was only about six or seven minutes after they had found Cameron, but it seemed like an eternity. He laid the boy carefully on the ground, pillowing his head with his own fleece jacket.

"He's in bad shape," Lucero said grimly, reaching into his pack full of first aid supplies to treat the boy. "Who knows how long he's been seizing? No doubt he's dehydrated and possibly hypothermic."

But he was alive. Cale knew that would have to be enough. They had him and he was alive.

While the paramedic worked quickly to try to stop the seizure, Cale finally picked up the field telephone to report, hoping the wires hadn't been damaged beyond repair by the cave-in.

"We've got the boy," he told the voice on the other end of the line after he had identified their team.

He heard an exultant cry go out from those who must have been in the room, and his throat felt tight imagining how Megan would react when she heard the news. "He's breathing but unconscious and needs medical attention immediately."

"Do you want a litter?"

"There's no time to wait for a team to bring one. We'll start bringing him out, and they can meet us on the way. Have a medical team and an ambulance standing by."

The journey out of the labyrinth would forever live in his memory as some of the most desperate moments of his life. Cameron still didn't respond to either him or Ben, though the boy appeared to have stopped convulsing. At least the terrible shudders were no longer racking his body, though Cam seemed frail and insubstantial in his arms.

They were still some way from the entrance when they encountered the incoming team with the litter.

Only after Cale had lowered the boy into it and relinquished his care to the other rescuers did he realize that every muscle in his body ached and that his shoulder throbbed as if somebody had shoved a frigging branding iron through it.

He didn't care. Cameron Vance was alive, and right now that was the only thing that mattered.

* * *

Megan sat in her kitchen, her hands folded tightly in her lap, and waited and waited and waited. She felt as if she had been sitting here forever, that her skin and bones had fused with the chair.

Cale had been in the mine for nearly three hours, and she didn't know how much more of this agony she could endure. She also wasn't sure which was more difficult—the endless night of uncertainty when she had no idea where her son might be, or this, knowing where Cameron probably was but being forced to wait here while others looked for him.

It didn't help that now she worried about two people—her son and an FBI agent she hadn't even known forty-eight hours earlier.

She couldn't seem to stop thinking about Cale Davis and his wounded eyes and his fierce determination to find her son.

She might be able to endure this endless vigil if only someone would tell her something—*anything*. But between the search and rescue operation for Cameron and the investigation into the drug lab and the dead body found in the mine, all the law enforcement personnel seemed far too busy to remember she was there.

She supposed she would rather have them all ignore her, if it meant they were focusing all their energies on finding her son.

Suddenly, her cell phone rang. Her nerves were so frayed that she jumped and nearly fell out of her chair. With trembling hands, she picked it up, then flipped it open when she recognized Molly's number.

"Hello?"

"What's going on up there? Have they found him?" Molly sounded as tense and as worried as Megan. "Scott's listening to the scanner, and he said they just called for an ambulance."

An ambulance! Megan jumped up and hurried to the kitchen window, as if she could see anything from here up on the mountainside. "I don't know. No one has said."

The words were barely out of her mouth before Gage McKinnon hurried into the room.

His expression was closed but she immediately picked up something different about him, a strange, tense energy vibrating off of him.

She drew in a shaky breath, not daring to acknowledge the bright, wild wings of hope flapping inside her.

"What's happened?" she asked him urgently.

"You need to come with me."

She heard Molly's sharp gasp in her ear but couldn't focus on anything but Agent McKinnon's hard blue eyes. "Did they find my son?"

He nodded, his features carefully impassive. "The conditions in there are very unstable. Cameron was almost caught in a cave-in, but Cale and his search partner were able to extract him just before the tunnel collapsed completely. They're bringing him out now."

"Oh, praise God. Praise God," Molly sobbed in her ear as Megan swayed and gripped the edge of the counter.

"How is he?"

"I have to be honest, at last report his condition was very guarded. He was seizing when Cale and his partner found him. They had to get him to a safe place before they could administer meds to stop the seizure. That's all I know at this point."

She rushed for the door without any conscious idea of her actions, driven only by the need to see her son, to touch his face, to hold him close and feel him breathe.

"I'll take you up, Mrs. Vance. I've got an ATV standing by."

She nodded and let Cale's partner lead the way.

Chapter 11

Cale had learned early in his time with the FBI—long before then, really, during his tense, miserable childhood—how to bury his emotions deep down, so far down he sometimes forgot they were there.

He couldn't do that on this case, no matter how hard he tried. As he carried the back end of the litter holding Cameron Vance out, a storm of emotions seemed to pour through him, and he didn't know quite how to sort them out.

There was definite relief they had found the boy, gratitude they had been in the right place at the right time to rescue him just before the chamber collapsed.

Coupled with that relief was a deep fear for the boy's health since Cameron still hadn't regained consciousness—though he seemed to have stopped convulsing and his breathing was stable.

Those were enough to contend with. But somehow finding Cameron seemed to have weathered away the flimsy barrier he had constructed around his psyche to keep what had happened two weeks earlier from consuming him. The two events had somehow come to mesh in his mind and he found himself reliving in gruesome detail those horrible moments after shooting Andy Decker, when he had stumbled into that cabin and found the girls.

He tried to block those images out, the long moments of trying to resuscitate the girls, but they seemed to come faster and faster.

The only way he could keep it together was to focus on the job at hand, on the tricky process of moving one boot in front of the other through the dark, uneven terrain and keeping the litter stabilized as they maneuvered through the labyrinth.

"One more left turn in about twenty feet, and then the entrance should be straight ahead," the rescuer in the lead said.

"You sure you don't want me to take over?" Lucero asked Cale.

"I've got it," he said. "You just keep doing your medic thing."

He had to see this through to the end. Cameron had come to mean far more to him than a case and he wanted to be there when the boy emerged from the hole into the sunlight, even if he was unconscious and didn't know the difference.

"How's he doing?" one of the other rescuers asked Lucero.

"The Diastat appears to have stopped the seizure. At this point, I think his unresponsive state is just postictal."

"What does that mean?" the man asked.

"After a big seizure, the brain sometimes decides to take a little holiday to recover for a while," Lucero explained as they moved slowly toward the light.

"A patient can fall into what appears to be a deep sleep and be hard to rouse. Not really unconscious, but close to it," he went on. "I would say the seizure on top of everything else the kid has been through in the last thirty-six hours was just too much for him and he's shut down on us for a while. I can't imagine what it would be like to be trapped in this darkness for a day and a half. It would be too much for most grown men I know."

Cale's hands tightened on the litter and he was astonished by the wave of tenderness washing through him for this child, a boy he had never even met.

"We managed to get the ambulance about fifty feet away from the mine entrance but that was as close as we dared go in the steep terrain," one of the other rescuers explained as they made the final turn. Light poured in through the entrance, and Cale decided that sunlight playing over the ground of the mine was the most beautiful thing he had ever seen.

"You boys okay carrying the litter the rest of the way or do you want somebody else to take over?" Lucero asked.

"I'm good," one said. "We've made it this far. I'm in for the distance."

"Davis?"

"Let's get him out of here," Cale answered. They moved the last few yards to the opening, then emerged from the mine.

An exultant cry went up from the crowd of searchers and rescue workers gathered there.

He blinked, disoriented by the rapid shift from Stygian darkness to the brilliance of an August afternoon in the Rockies. His eyes hadn't adjusted yet, but he was still aware of a small shape disengaging from the crowd.

"Stop," Cale ordered the other rescuers carrying the litter. They froze as Megan rushed to the litter, sobbing tears of relief.

"Cam! Oh, Cameron!" She grabbed his hand, clutching it to her breast tightly.

It had taken them at least an hour to get the boy out of the mine and he had been unresponsive the entire time. At the sound of his mother's voice, though, Cameron's eyes fluttered open.

"Mommy?" he croaked.

Megan gave a sobbing little laugh. "I'm here, baby. I'm here."

The boy's features lifted into a smile, then he closed his eyes again.

"He's postictal, ma'am," Lucero explained. "And probably plain worn out."

Megan didn't seem to mind. She held his hand tight, wiping away tears with her other hand. The men carrying the litter started down the hill toward the waiting ambulance.

It was a little tough going with Megan still clinging to her son's hand, but Cale didn't think any of the rescuers minded.

He certainly didn't mind. She was only a few feet in front of him and he couldn't help thinking she seemed different from the fragile, heartsick woman he had met during the last day and a half.

This woman glowed from the inside out. She was so beautiful he couldn't look away.

The adrenaline carried all of them through the ten minutes it took to carefully transport the litter on a steep angle to the waiting ambulance. At last they lifted Cam into the ambulance. Megan started to climb in, then she paused on the step, surveying the rescuers.

Though her gaze encompassed all of them, she seemed to stop on Cale. A warmth kindled there, a subtle, tensile connection between them and he wanted desperately to pull her into his arms.

"Thank you. Words can never be enough to express my gratitude for what you have all done. Thank you." She swiped away tears, and Cale saw more than one big, burly rescuer doing the same. She gave them all a tremulous smile then climbed in after her son.

He stood and watched the ambulance drive down the mountain. The sides of the road were thronged with cameras and news vans and the hundreds of volunteers who had turned out to help look for Cameron. When the ambulance passed, everyone started clapping and cheering and hugging each other.

As he watched Megan ride away with her son, the hard, bleak knot around his chest seemed to break free, and he sucked in what felt like the first clean, pure breath of air in weeks.

"Hey, Davis, you're bleeding," Lucero said, a concerned note in his voice. "You get caught on a rock or something?"

Cale looked down and was baffled to see blood

soaking through his shirt. Not just a little blood, either. He drew in another breath as the adrenaline high began to seep away and he suddenly became aware of jagged pain radiating from his shoulder, pain he must have suppressed during the rescue.

Damn. He must have broken through his stitches.

She couldn't seem to let go of her son.

Megan sat with Cameron's small, battered hand clutched tightly in both of hers in the tastefully decorated treatment room at the small Moose Springs medical clinic while Dr. Maxwell finished her exam.

Cam had only opened his eyes a few times in the hour since he'd been pulled out of the cave and hadn't said anything beyond the few words when he had seen her.

She was trying not to worry about his continued unresponsiveness, but it wasn't easy.

The doctor pulled her stethoscope away from her ears and draped them around her neck before she pulled the warm blankets back up around Cameron.

"You've got a tough kid there, Megan," Lauren Maxwell said as she made a notation on his chart.

She had always known he was strong—he handled the tests and special diet and hospital stays due to his epilepsy with patience and equanimity. But she had to think Cameron had reserves she'd never even guessed at to survive such an ordeal.

"He's still so out of it. You think he's still postictal or is there more to it?"

"That's my guess. All his vitals look great, especially after we started the IV fluids. We don't know how long he was seizing before the rescuers found him. I think the combination of that nasty seizure and the ordeal he's been through must have sapped the last of his strength. We're just fortunate they found him when they did."

She shivered. A few more moments and the tunnel Cameron was in would have collapsed while he was suffering a major seizure. Sheriff Galvez had been by already and told her in more detail what had happened, that Cale and another searcher had risked their lives to pull her son out of the darkness.

She couldn't bear thinking how close she had come to losing her little boy forever, to never knowing what had become of him.

"I'm confident he'll start coming back to us," Lauren went on. "All he needs is a little time to rest and recover."

"I hope so."

The doctor looked at her out of concerned blue eyes. "I would give the exact same prescription to his mother. Believe it or not, that chair you're sitting on folds out into a bed. It's about as comfortable as sleeping on a concrete slab, but I imagine right now you wouldn't even notice."

It was silly, she knew, but she didn't want to leave Cam's side, even to stretch out on a chair a few feet away.

"I'm all right," she assured the doctor, thinking how much she liked and admired the other woman.

Though she had heard whispers about Lauren's past from a few malicious people in town in the few months she had been in Moose Springs, Megan didn't pay much attention.

She preferred to judge people by their actions and behavior and the doctor had been wonderfully kind to her and her children. She seemed to be an excellent doctor who cared deeply for her patients. Megan put more credence in that than in any rumors.

"Let my nurse know if you change your mind," Lauren said. "I'll be busy for a while stitching up one of the rescuers, but I'll come back to check on you and Cam later. I'd like to see you both sleeping."

Her attention caught on the first part of the doctor's statement. "Oh, dear. I hadn't heard one of the men had been injured during the search. Is he all right?"

Lauren's elegant features pulled into a frown. "Only stubborn and thickheaded. He wasn't in any condition to be in that mine in the first place, not when he was nursing a pre-existing injury. During the rescue effort, apparently he broke through some stitches and just needs to be sewn back up. He should be fine, though."

"Stitches?" She suddenly felt cold, and her hand clenched around Cameron's. Her mind flashed to her conversation with Gage McKinnon, and somehow she knew. "From a gunshot wound?"

Lauren's gaze narrowed. "Yeah. How did you know that?"

She mustered a smile, though she ached inside to know Cale had been hurt again on her son's behalf. "Because I know the stubborn, thickheaded man in question. If not for him, Cameron wouldn't be here. Please take good care of him."

Lauren's mouth quirked into a lopsided smile. "All right. Since you asked so nicely, I guess I won't sew him up using dirty twine and a used needle."

Too late, she realized how her words must have been construed. "Oh! I'm sorry, I didn't mean..."

"Megan, I'm joking. It's okay. Cale is a friend. I

promise, I would be gentle with him even if he wasn't the hero of the hour."

She had a difficult time picturing Cale in social situations. Did he lose that bleakness in his eyes when he was around friends? she wondered. Did his smile reach those eyes? She hoped so, for his sake.

After Lauren left, she shifted position in the chair, trying to find a comfortable spot. Her entire body ached from the sleepless night and the long, torturous hours of worry.

She owed Cale so much. He had worked doggedly to find her son. She knew he had tracked down lead after lead. He had sat beside her in the night, had comforted her and lifted her when she was beginning to feel as if all hope were lost.

He was the only person to think of asking Hailey about her brother's whereabouts.

And he had gone into that mine despite his own injury and had been willing to lay down his life to bring her son home.

Megan owed him *everything*.

Her chest ached with a combination of gratitude, awed respect and soft, poignant tenderness.

She stiffened, her fingers tightening around Cameron's. Tenderness? How had he become so vitally important to her in such a short time? A few days ago she hadn't even met Caleb, so how could she possibly feel as if her life would be terribly empty without him?

This was ridiculous. She had no business feeling anything for a battle-scarred lawman like Cale Davis.

"Mommy?"

She pushed away the terrifying feelings and shifted

attention to her son, exactly where her focus should be. "I'm here, Cam. Right here."

His pupils were still large, and he blinked at her like a baffled little bird. "It's not dark anymore."

It was the most he had said since he had been carried out of the mine, and she had to work hard to keep the tears from her voice. "No, baby. You're safe now."

He frowned, tugging at his blanket with restless little motions. "I have to tell…"

He closed his eyes as Megan waited for him to gather the energy to complete the sentence. After a moment, she realized she would likely be waiting for a while as he had apparently fallen asleep again.

She smoothed the blond hair from his eyes, her heart tight and achy with love and relief.

"Just rest, sweetheart," she murmured, in the same voice she used when he was a baby falling asleep in her arms.

She knew he was already asleep and couldn't hear her words of comfort, but she said them anyway. "I'm not going anywhere. You can tell us everything when you wake up."

He shouldn't be here.

Cale stood outside Cameron Vance's room at the clinic, wondering if he ought to just catch a ride back to the city and put this whole thing behind him.

His job was done in Moose Springs. The boy was safe and sound in his mother's arms, and a rogue FBI agent on his acting boss's hit list should probably be hustling back to work, trying to preserve whatever was left of his career. Not hovering in the hallway working up the nerve to go inside and say goodbye to a woman and boy who had changed everything.

Yet here he stood.

He let out a breath, then winced at the pinch in the new sutures Lauren Maxwell had just put in so carefully.

Trouble was, the job didn't *feel* done. Yeah, Cameron was out of the mine, but Cale knew he was far from safe. The boy had seen Wally Simon's murder. Cale would stake his life on it.

Cameron was a witness, a witness who would be in grave danger if he could identify the killer.

Even if he *couldn't* identify the killer, he was in danger. The shooter wouldn't know whether Cam had seen him or not.

Word was already out that the missing boy had been found in the mine. With national media coverage on every station, whoever whacked the meth cook would have to connect the dots and figure out the boy had gone missing at approximately the same time as the murder had occurred.

He needed to warn Megan, to give her all the information at hand so she could be prepared to protect her son from any possible threat. That was the reason he was standing out here, he told himself.

It had nothing to do with this fierce need inside him to see her soft, fragile features one more time, to make sure for himself that she and Cameron were both all right.

Cale sighed. Right. Who was he kidding? Not himself, certainly.

He raised his hand to knock on the door but before he could, it opened and startled green eyes flashed to his.

The surprise in them quickly changed to something else, a jumble of emotions he couldn't begin to sort out.

"Cale!" she exclaimed. Her voice was pitched low and over her shoulder he could see Cameron sleeping peacefully in the bed.

"Hey."

He could drown in those eyes, he thought. Especially when they softened with a sweet concern that took his breath away.

"How are you?" she asked, holding the door open for him to come inside the room.

He couldn't seem to take his eyes off her. She seemed different, somehow. He couldn't figure it out for a moment, then he realized that for the first time, he was seeing her free of the paralyzing worry for her son's safety. His heart swelled and he wanted to pull her into his arms. It took all his energy to fight the urge.

"Doctor Maxwell told me you broke your stitches open during the rescue and she had to sew you up," she said after a pause.

She pitched her voice low, so he did likewise. "Yeah. She just finished up. It's no big deal."

"Don't say that. It's a *huge* deal." She touched his arm, and he could swear he felt the heat of her through the cotton of his shirt. "I feel terrible, knowing you were hurt rescuing Cameron. I'm so very sorry you were hurt again."

He shook his head. *He* wasn't sorry. "That mine was exactly where I needed to be today."

"I'm sorry you were hurt," she said again. "But I can't honestly say I'm sorry you were there, even though I know I probably should. If not for you, Cam wouldn't be here. I can never thank you enough."

Her chin wobbled a little, and she seemed to be fighting for control. It was too much for him, more than he could handle after the dramatic emotions of the day.

With a sigh of defeat, he reached for her and pulled her into his arms.

Chapter 12

She was perfect in his arms, soft and warm and womanly, all the things he had been telling himself he could manage without.

With a sigh, she slid her arms around his waist and rested her head against his chest. Something hard and cold inside him seemed to crack apart, leaving only sweet, healing peace.

He wanted to close his eyes and hang on for the rest of his life.

"I owe you everything," she repeated. "Thank you for returning my son to me."

"You don't have to thank me," he said, his voice gruff. She smelled divine, of vanilla and cinnamon, like hot, sticky sweet rolls just out of the oven, dripping with icing, and he was suddenly starving.

"Nothing I do could ever repay you for what you have done," she murmured.

This was a pretty darn good start. He would feel fully compensated if she would only let him stand here holding her for the next five or ten years, with her warmth surrounding him and the delicious scent of her filling up his senses.

"I needed to find him," he admitted after a moment. "I had to be in those tunnels today. I can't explain all the reasons why, even to myself, but I had no choice. It was something I had to do."

She was quiet for a moment, even as her arms tightened around him. "Because of what happened to the Decker girls?" she finally asked.

He froze, then let out a ragged breath, grateful she couldn't see the raw pain he knew would be obvious in his eyes. "You know about that?"

Her soft, gilt-tipped hair brushed his chin when she nodded. "Your partner told me this morning. I'm sorry, Caleb."

"Five minutes earlier—hell, two minutes—and I could have saved them. Every time I think of those brief seconds, I can't breathe and feel like my heart is being sliced apart."

He hadn't told anyone that, not even the FBI shrink he'd been ordered to see after the incident. Yet he wanted Megan to know that piece of himself, the depth of his pain and guilt.

Her arms tightened around him. "Don't do this to yourself. Please don't. I know you, Caleb Davis. I have seen your dedication to your job firsthand. That boy asleep on that bed over there is all the evidence I need. I am one hundred percent convinced you did everything humanly possible to save those girls. Don't spend the rest of your life blaming yourself for something a sick, twisted man did to his own children."

To his horror, his eyes burned with unshed tears. He blinked them back fiercely, trying to hang on to control.

How long it had been since he had cried? He couldn't remember. Probably that day he was twelve years old and had to hear about his sister's death in such a cold, public way.

He tightened his arms around Megan, stunned to his core to feel the darkness begin to lift, to feel the healing touch of light.

She was right. Absolutely right. Everything Megan said to him had been said by others since he had been shot. By Gage, by the Bureau shrink, even by the girls' mother. After that first wild outcry, she had assured him she didn't blame him for her daughters' deaths. She had come to his hospital room, and thanked him for trying so hard to save them.

So why did he continue to blame himself?

He wouldn't, he vowed. He knew he would always grieve for Soshi and Mirabel Decker, and their names would always be etched in his heart. He would probably always feel some guilt that he hadn't been able to save them. But he had realized, emerging from the bleak darkness of the mine today, that he needed sunshine and light in his life.

He needed this woman in his arms.

He drew in a sharp breath as the realization poured through him, stunning and unavoidable.

"I must be hurting you," she said, easing away from him a little.

"The only way you could hurt me right now would be to let go," he confessed.

Her gaze flashed to his. He saw shock there and something else, a blooming awareness, like mountain wildflowers on a soft summer morning opening up for the sun.

Her lips parted slightly, only a few inches away from his, and he didn't think about their surroundings or the fact that her son slept just a few feet away. He couldn't help himself; he leaned forward and brushed his mouth against hers.

At first she froze in his arms, her mouth slack, and he thought—feared—she would pull away and take her warmth and her sweetness with her.

After a moment, she seemed to take a shuddering little breath, and her mouth moved under his in soft, subtle welcome as her arms tightened around him.

He slid into the kiss, forgetting the tight ache in his shoulder, the exhaustion in his muscles, the hard, heavy weight he had carried for two weeks. All of that seemed to drift away like falling leaves on a warm swirl of current and the only thing that mattered was Megan.

This couldn't be happening.

Some corner of her mind told her she shouldn't be doing this, kissing Caleb Davis, a man she barely knew. But his kiss was so tender, so breathtakingly sweet, and she was helpless to resist it.

In his arms, all the stress and fear of the last two days seemed like a distant memory and she wanted to stay right here, safe from the ugly world outside.

Her arms tightened around him and she was aware of the hard, muscled strength beneath her fingers, of his heat searing through her, warming places inside her that had been frozen solid for so terribly long.

She didn't want it to end, but that strident voice in her mind was already raising objections when she heard a knock at the door.

Oh, mercy. What was she thinking? She sprang away from him, breathing hard, just as Lauren Maxwell walked into the room.

The doctor paused in the doorway, her lovely features twisted into a startled expression before she quickly concealed it.

Could she guess what they had been doing an instant before? Oh, she hoped not. What would Lauren think of her?

Megan knew she must look flustered and unsettled. Her skin felt hot and prickly, and she knew she must be beet red. She was one of those unfortunate redheads whose skin showed every flicker of emotion, and right now she was blushing, inside and out.

She wanted to press her face into her hands, to curl up in the fetal position on the floor and yank one of Cameron's warmed blankets over her head.

"How is he?" the doctor asked.

She flushed brighter, then let out a breath, reminding herself the doctor was talking about Cameron, not Cale Davis and his tender kisses.

"He…he seems to be fine. The monitors haven't beeped once."

Megan could only be grateful *she* hadn't been the one hooked up to those monitors because she imagined that kiss would have set off a whole cacophony of alerts.

"Good. Do you need anything?"

Only a brain. And perhaps a cold shower. She shook her head. "I think we're fine in here."

"Cale? What about you?"

"Uh, no."

Megan took some small comfort that he sounded as disconcerted and off balance as she felt by their kiss.

"How's the shoulder? Is the local wearing off?"

"It's fine. Thanks again for the patch job."

"I would tell you anytime, but I don't want you to take me up on it. I'd rather not have to stitch up my friends."

He gave a crooked smile, and Megan wondered if their relationship had ever been more than just friends. No, she wasn't picking up any kind of vibe like that between the two of them.

"You mind if I take a look at Cameron?" Lauren asked.

"Of course not." She moved aside as the doctor walked to the bedside, pulling out Cam's chart and making a notation in it.

Cale took one of the chairs in the room, but Megan chose to remain standing, fighting the urge to cover her face with her hands.

What had she been thinking to kiss him that way, and with her son sleeping only a few feet away? she wondered.

The physical attraction wasn't so surprising, she supposed. What woman wouldn't be drawn to Cale's lean, masculine features, those stunning polar-blue eyes or the soft dark hair that begged for a woman to twist her fingers through it?

It was a normal physiological response to a gorgeous man. She didn't like it, though she could certainly understand it.

But what really scared her was the emotional tug between them.

Somehow in the last day and a half, he had become important to her, had managed to sneak past her defenses and make himself at home.

How could she have let it happen? She wasn't ready for this. She didn't want it. Absolutely not.

Even if she *were* ready to jump into something, she certainly wouldn't let herself fall for a man like Caleb Davis. If she ever allowed herself to care for another man, he would be someone solid. Someone dependable and settled and *safe*.

She knew what it was like to sit at home waiting for someone who was busy saving the world. She knew the loneliness and the fear, the heartache and the uncertainty.

It took a special kind of courage to love a warrior, and Megan was afraid she had used up a lifetime's worth being married to Rick.

She knew her husband had loved his job and she had tried to be supportive. But she had died a little inside every time he went out on a mission, afraid this would be the one that would take him from her.

She couldn't live through that again. She *wouldn't*.

Cale was an FBI agent, a man completely dedicated to his job, as well. She knew he must take risks, that he put himself in danger for those he served. If she needed proof, she only had to look at his bloody shirt that covered a half-healed gunshot wound right now.

She couldn't be foolish enough to jump headlong into that kind of pain and fear again.

Even though she was powerfully drawn to him on both a physical and emotional level, she would just have to do her best to ignore it. A smart woman learned to stay away from things that were bad for her, and right now Caleb Davis topped her personal list.

His arms had felt wonderful around her, though, warm and strong and comforting.

A shiver coursed through her, and she was grateful Caleb and Dr. Maxwell seemed focused on Cameron, just where Megan's attention should be.

Her son's eyes were opening again, she realized, and she hurried to his side as they fluttered all the way open.

"Mom?" he said, his voice raspy.

"Right here, honey." She picked up his hand.

"My head hurts. What happened?"

He sounded so *normal*, just like a nine-year-old boy waking up tired and achy and cranky, that she had to choke back a sob of relief. Every time he had a seizure, especially the bad ones, her deepest fear was that the irregular brain activity would somehow steal away more of him.

"What do you remember?" she asked.

"I was trapped in the dark and couldn't find my way out. Thirsty. Scared."

"You're safe now."

He closed his eyes for a moment. She thought he might have drifted off, but then they fluttered open again. "Are you mad at me?" he asked, a fearful note in his voice.

Deep in her heart, she wanted to hug him and hold him and tell him of course she wasn't mad, that she could never be mad at him, especially since she had him in her arms again.

But she knew she couldn't let him off that easily, not when he had taken such foolish risks and put himself and so many others in danger.

Parenting was hard business, especially when her soft mommy side that wanted to kiss him and tell him everything would be all right warred with the harsh, realistic side that knew she would be doing him no favors if she didn't stress the consequences to his actions.

"Yes, I'm mad," she told him firmly. "You were wrong to sneak out in the middle of the night and you know better than to go into an abandoned mine by yourself."

Cameron looked glum until she finally gave in to that maternal side and pulled him into her arms. He snuggled against her, and she had to fight back tears when she thought of those long hours when she feared this moment wouldn't come.

"I am very upset that you broke our family rules and put yourself and others in such danger."

She touched his small, dear face. "But I'm also so very, very happy that you were found and that you're safe."

He blinked a little, then smiled. After a moment, his eyes drifted closed again and she felt his body relax in her arms.

"He's aware enough to worry about his mom being mad at him," Cale spoke up from the corner. She had almost—not quite—forgotten he was there. "I'd say that's a good sign, wouldn't you, Lauren?"

The doctor smiled. "A very good sign. We'll have to wait to see how things go for the next few hours. But given his encouraging vitals, I don't see any reason you can't take him home later and try to get some sleep in your own bed."

At her words, Megan realized how deeply exhausted she was, how every part of her ached with fatigue. She wanted to sink into sleep right there, sitting on the edge of her son's hospital bed. Even as she fought to keep her eyes open, she was aware of Cale's troubled expression.

He didn't say anything while Lauren finished making some adjustments to the IV pump. "I'll check back in fifteen minutes or so," the doctor said, then slipped from the room.

When she was gone, Cale rose and came to stand beside her. "I don't want you to be alone at home right now. Is there someone who can stay with you?"

She raised an eyebrow at his imperious tone. Why hadn't she noticed how bossy he was before? Still another reason to keep him at the top of her things-to-avoid-even-though-she-wanted-them list.

"We'll be fine," she said.

"I know you're happy to have Cameron back and you want to go home as soon as possible so you can try to return to the life you had before. But this isn't over. You need to consider what's at stake here."

She frowned. "What do you mean?"

"A man was murdered in that mine. If my hunch is right, Cameron may have seen it go down. It's possible he can identify the shooter—and even if he can't, just the fact that he was in the mine at approximately the same time as the murder could put him in grave jeopardy."

Her arms tightened around her son's sleeping form. She didn't want to hear this. That dead body they found in the mine seemed so distant, almost unrelated to her missing son.

She had been so totally focused on finding Cameron she had paid it little mind. Hearing Caleb's stark assessment of the situation and seeing his continuing unease was a forceful reminder to her that all was not perfect for her son.

"I think you need to stay with your sister for the night. Or barring that, you need to have someone stay at your house to keep an eye on things until we know Cameron's side of the story."

"What about you?"

The moment the words escaped her, she regretted them and wished more than anything to call them back. She didn't want to spend more time with Caleb Davis. She needed distance from the man, time to rebuild the barricades he had smashed through.

Beyond that, hadn't he given enough? The man had been awake for nearly forty-eight hours, had spent most of the day in the dark and dank, had risked his life.

She couldn't ask more of him.

"I'm sorry. Forget I said that. We will be fine. I have an excellent security system and with all the media still camped out down the street, we'll be perfectly safe."

"I'm sure you will," he answered. "Because I'll be there to make certain of it."

She opened her mouth to argue, then closed it again and let the matter ride, too tired to work up the energy.

She had been the one to suggest it, after all. How could she now tell him that, upon further reflection, she opposed the idea, simply because she didn't trust herself in the same room with him?

Four hours later, Cale stood in Cameron Vance's sports-decorated bedroom gazing with frustration at the boy's stubborn mother as she pulled up a chair and settled in beside him.

"You can't sit here all night, Megan. You haven't slept in two days." Her eyes were so shadowed they looked like big angry bruises. A few more moments and she was going to fall over. He only hoped he would still be awake to catch her.

"I can't leave him," she murmured. "I just can't. Not yet. But you don't need to stay up with us. There's a guest room two doors down on the left. Get some rest. You've been up as long as I have."

From the doorway, he gazed at her for a long moment—that soft, feathery hair, the delicate curve of her features, the slender arch of her neck as she looked down at her son. How had this slight, fragile woman and her well-being become so terribly important to him in such a short time?

A terrifying tenderness surged up inside him like a wellspring and he was very much afraid it was far too late to do anything about capping it.

He sighed and turned to go, but her voice stopped him.

"Caleb. Thank you again," she said softly. "I do feel better knowing you're here."

He managed a smile, knowing it was a hard concession for her to offer. She hadn't wanted him to spend the night. She had told him so in no uncertain terms, and he couldn't blame her. She wanted her house back, her privacy, her life. How could he begrudge her that?

But he also couldn't shake this unease for Cameron's safety. Until they had a suspect in custody for the Simon murder, he knew Cameron was in danger.

That didn't mean the boy's mother had to sit up all night. He went in search of supplies and returned a few moments later. Her eyes widened at the load in his arms.

"What's this?"

He set the pile of bedding he had raided from the

guest room on a nearby dresser. "You've got to be at least as tired as I am. Cam's not going anywhere tonight."

He pulled the thick comforter off the pile and folded it into a bedroll. It would at least give her a little padding on the floor. He laid it beside Cameron's bed, then topped it with the pillow and another blanket.

"There you go. Now you can stretch out here and be close if he wakes up."

She looked stunned, as if he had just handed her the keys to her own private island, a hundred servants and a luxury yacht to take her there.

"I...thank you," she mumbled.

She lifted her green eyes toward his and to his horror, he spied a tear trickling down her cheek.

"Ah, damn. I'm sorry. Don't cry."

He wanted desperately to hold her, but he had seen the shock and dismay in her eyes at the hospital after he had been stupid enough to kiss her. He wasn't eager to get that reaction again, though it was killing him not to pull her into his arms.

"I'm the one who's sorry. We've been such a bother to you." She gave him a watery smile and he could only stare at her, rattled to the depths of his soul by the sudden inescapable truth.

He was in love with her.

He drew in a sharp breath, totally stunned. He didn't know how it had possibly happened in such a short time and under such terrible circumstances, but he couldn't deny it.

He might desperately want to pretend it was just a result of exhaustion and stress but he knew he would be lying to himself, something he tried not to do on a regular basis.

He was in love with Megan Vance, a woman still grieving for her hero of a husband, a woman he had only kissed once, to a less-than-stellar reception.

Okay. Probably not the smartest move he'd ever made.

"Get some sleep," he managed. His voice came out gruff, but he hoped she would blame it on fatigue.

"Right. You, too. Thank you, Caleb. For the bedroll and for…everything else."

He didn't want her gratitude, but he was very much afraid that was all he would ever have. "You're welcome. Good night."

He left quickly, closing the door tight behind him, then stood in the hallway for a long time, his mind buzzing with shock and no small amount of dismay.

In love with her. How the hell had he let it happen? Yes, he had come to care about her these last few days and found much to admire in her response to tremendous adversity.

She had survived the nightmare of the last two days with courage and strength, showing incredible grace and compassion toward him even when she was dealing with her own crippling fear.

He respected her and had come to care about her. But *love*. That was something else entirely.

He didn't know the first thing about being in love. He figured since it hadn't hit him yet by the ripe old age of thirty-five, he must have dodged that particular bullet.

He had always told himself he preferred being alone, that he wasn't cut out for anything else.

Now he wanted more, with a hunger that just about sent him to his knees. He wanted what Rick Vance had lost. He wanted Megan and Cameron and Hailey.

He rubbed a fist to the ache in his chest, knowing the fierce yearning was impossible. Megan didn't return his feelings. He hadn't needed to see her reaction to their kiss to know that.

After a moment, he sighed and slid to the floor of the hallway. He would have to figure out how to go on from here, how to live the rest of his life with this aching void in his heart. But not right now. For this moment, his only concern was keeping her safe.

Chapter 13

She hadn't meant to sleep. She didn't want to leave her son even for a moment, even to surrender to the demands of her body. But the last two days had been so traumatic and exhausting, she couldn't fight the inevitable. The moment she stretched out on a pallet on the floor, she must have drifted off.

She awoke some time later to moonlight streaming through the windows, washing everything a pale, pearly gray.

In that hazy moment between sleep and wakefulness, panic suddenly exploded through her like a brushfire in a hot wind and she blinked her eyes open.

Cam! She had to find Cameron!

She jumped up, disoriented as to why she was on the floor, and then she saw the source of her panic stretched out on his bed, his soccer ball comforter pulled up to his shoulders.

She instantly remembered the last two harrowing days—the frantic search for him, the long, agonizing hours of waiting, then the stunning joy of knowing he was safe.

Needing reassurance, she couldn't keep from reaching out to touch the hand that had slipped from his covers, just to make sure he was really there. She relaxed at the feel of warm skin and stood by the bed gazing down at her son and forcing her breathing to slow.

Though he wanted to be a rough-and-tumble boy and she tried hard to treat him as such, Cameron had always seemed fragile to her.

He was three when he had his first seizure. His epilepsy and the special medical needs stemming from it had become routine over the years, but sometimes she still wanted to wrap him in layers of cotton and keep him close to her to protect him from the dangers both inside and outside his body.

She supposed it was normal to want to coddle him. But she needed to remember Cameron had a deep reservoir of strength she never would have guessed at. He must, or he would never have been able to survive his ordeal in the mine.

She sighed, fighting the urge to gather him in her arms. It was selfish to wake him just because she needed reassurance. Instead, she sat on the edge of the bed watching him breathe and wondering how she could ever let him out of her sight again.

After a moment, her stomach growled loudly enough so that Cameron stirred and then rolled over.

Could she actually be hungry, for the first time in two

days? She hadn't even wanted to think about food while Cam was missing and hadn't eaten more than a bite or two throughout that terrible time. No wonder she was starving.

The kitchen was full of food, she remembered. Brimming over, actually, with all the food neighbors had brought over. Her stomach growled again, just thinking about it.

She hated to leave Cameron even for a moment, but she could hurry down and raid the kitchen for a sandwich, then bring it back here to eat, she decided.

After checking one more time to make sure Cameron still slept peacefully, she turned on the closet light so he wouldn't wake up in the dark.

Her mind on her stomach, she opened the bedroom door—and nearly tripped over a body sprawled in the hall.

She swallowed a scream as the figure jerked up.

"What is it? What's wrong?" In the pale light from the closet, she could just make out Cale's features. Though she must have awakened him from a sound sleep, he clicked immediately to full alertness, like some kind of wild predator.

Inside the room, Cameron stirred but didn't awaken. Megan closed the door behind her most of the way, leaving it open a crack. The only light now came from the star-shaped night-light she kept burning near the stairs.

"What are you doing here?" she hissed.

He raked his fingers through his hair, further tangling the dark strands that were already mussed. "Having the daylights scared out of me, apparently."

"Why are you sleeping on the floor? I told you how to find the guest room, didn't I?"

"You did." He stood and stretched, all hard, lean

muscles and gorgeous masculinity, and she had to swallow hard as painful awareness bloomed inside her that they were virtually alone in her darkened house at three in the morning.

She cleared her throat. "So, uh, tell me why you aren't sleeping in the guest room."

"I wanted to be close, just in case."

She couldn't seem to make her hazy brain function. Whether that was a byproduct of waking up after only a few disjointed hours of sleep or had more to do with the man standing in front of her all sleep-rumpled and sexy, she didn't want to hazard a guess.

"In case what?" she asked.

A shrug was his only answer, and it took several seconds for the truth to soak through her befuddled mind.

He was there to watch over them.

She could only stare at him, a strange warmth pouring through her. He was recovering from a gunshot wound, he hadn't slept in two days and he had spent hours underground in the dirt and darkness looking for her son. Yet he was willing to take what little sleep he could find on the hard floor of her hallway outside her son's bedroom in order to keep them safe.

How could she possibly resist a man who would do such a thing?

"You think Cam's in that much danger that you have to stand vigil through the night?" she asked when she could trust her voice.

"Maybe not. I may be completely overreacting."

"But you don't think so."

"I think we're going to have to wait to gauge the extent of the risk until we know what happened in there.

In the meantime, this is one of those better-safe-than-sorry situations."

His soberness unnerved her; at the same time, she was touched to the depths of her soul by his concern. She couldn't help herself; she extended a hand and touched his arm.

"I wish you didn't feel like you have to sleep on the floor, but I'm glad you're here," she murmured.

After a pause, he covered her hand with his. She could feel the hard strength of his fingers on top of her hand and the warm skin of his arm beneath. "So am I."

In the dim light of the night-light, she thought she saw something leap into his gaze, something hot and enticing. She drew in a shaky breath, suddenly remembering his kiss and the way she had wanted to burrow into him and stay there forever.

What was it about this man that drew her so powerfully? He only had to hold her hand and she lost all sense of reason and control.

She was in danger of falling hard for him.

The thought stole her breath, dousing her like a hard, cold rain. Oh mercy. What was she doing here?

She couldn't seem to make her muscles work and wanted to weep with gratitude when he pulled away first, returning his hand to the back pocket of his jeans.

"Where were you going when I so rudely interrupted you with my legs?" he asked.

She followed his lead and tried to adopt a casualness she was far from feeling, especially given the stunning depth of emotion she wasn't at all ready to acknowledge.

"I was, uh, hungry, believe it or not."

She stepped away, desperately needing more space

between them. "I thought I would head down to the kitchen to grab a sandwich. I would be happy to fix you one if you're interested."

"Now that you mention it, I am a little hungry. But you don't have to fix something for me. I can do it."

She needed to escape him, if only for a moment, so she could try to regain a little balance and talk some sense into herself. "I don't mind. Why don't you stay here in case Cameron wakes up?"

He studied her in the dim light; she fervently hoped he couldn't read anything in her expression. "Sure," he said finally, and she hurried away as fast as she could without breaking into a panicked run.

The house seemed oddly unfamiliar to her as she moved down the stairs to the kitchen. She and the children had only lived here a few months, but that didn't fully explain how disorienting it seemed to walk through the darkened rooms.

Perhaps it was because in some strange but fundamental way, the ordeal of the last two days had changed her. She wasn't the same woman who had awakened in the middle of the night to find her son gone. That seemed another lifetime ago. A dozen lifetimes.

As she expected, she found the kitchen bulging with food, offering dozens of choices. The sight of it all touched her, reminding her of early days after Rick's death when her neighbors and friends had filled her larder to overflowing.

Food was the eternal panacea. The physical act of eating did little to ease the grief, she knew, but the caring and love that went into preparing the food could provide great comfort.

She stood in front of the refrigerator, struck by the mortifying realization that she had been so flustered upstairs that she hadn't bothered to ask Cale what kind of sandwich he preferred.

Somehow her failure seemed to steady her. It was a silly thing, but she reassured herself that she couldn't possibly be falling in love with a man when she didn't have the first idea what kind of sandwich he favored.

She would just make him an assortment, she decided. She found packages of ham and turkey deli meat, as well as some cheese slices, in the refrigerator. Working quickly, she made two of each, then threw in a humble peanut butter and jelly, just in case.

Someone had brought over a pasta salad that looked delicious, and she found a bowl of fresh fruit on the table still in plastic wrap. She pulled out a couple of apples, then added several thick, chewy brownies from a heaping plate.

It was too much food—a feast that would feed a small crowd—but she set everything on a tray anyway, adding two bottles of water.

At the top of the stairs, she found Cale had turned on the lamp in the small area on the landing that overlooked the two-story great room. She used this for a reading nook, and it was one of her favorite spaces in the house.

"I figured this was a good place for a midnight snack," he said.

It was down the hall from Cameron's room, but not too far they couldn't hear him if he awakened.

She mustered a smile. "We're about three hours past a midnight snack, but I suppose you can still call it that."

He smiled in return and for a long moment, she could

do nothing but stare. She hadn't seen him smile much. She never would have expected to find it so devastating.

Oh, she was in grave trouble here. She set the bulging tray on the low coffee table, resisting the urge to drop the whole thing and run back to Cameron's room where she could bar the door against this man who made her feel things she had never wanted to again.

"I didn't know what kind of sandwich you wanted." It seemed important that she make that point clear to him.

"Right now it wouldn't much matter. I'm hungry enough to eat anything you've got."

"Turkey or ham or PB & J."

"You choose what you want and I'll eat whatever's left."

After a slight hesitation, she picked up one of the turkey sandwiches and set it on the paper plate she had included on the tray, then watched carefully as he went for the ham.

It was ridiculous to even notice, she told herself. The man's sandwich preferences were none of her business and never would be.

They ate in silence for a moment. She couldn't remember a meal that tasted so deliciously satisfying. Perhaps it was because she had been so long without sustenance, but every bite seemed to burst with flavor.

Maybe that was the reason she had reacted so strongly to his kiss, to his touch. She had been alone for two years now. Maybe she was just susceptible to the first gorgeous man who came along.

No, that couldn't be it. She had been asked out several times since Rick's death, both back in San Diego and in the few months since she had arrived in Moose Springs.

None of those other men had even sparked the tiniest flicker of interest in her and she had turned them all down.

She had responded to Cale because she cared about him. She was drawn to his strength and his compassion, his passionate dedication to his job, the glimpses of vulnerability he tried to hide.

He had slipped under her defenses somehow, had taken up root in her heart. She sighed, wondering how she was ever going to find the strength to push him away.

"Something wrong?" he asked.

Only everything.

Her instincts warned her to just make something up in reply, but she couldn't seem to think of anything but him. She knew why she responded to him so powerfully, but his motives were a mystery and she was suddenly burning to know.

"Can I ask you a question?"

"Sure. If you can get me to stop eating long enough to answer."

Even as the words formed, she knew pressing forward with this would be a huge mistake but she couldn't seem to stop herself.

"Why did you kiss me?"

Cale slowly chewed a bite of sandwich and swallowed, feeling a lot like he'd just been slammed by the entire Denver Broncos defensive line.

How was he supposed to answer that? If he told her the truth—that he was falling in love with her—she was bound to think he was crazy. *He* certainly thought he must be skipping a few gears.

"The, uh, usual reasons," he muttered.

Unfortunately, she wasn't going to let him get away with that kind of cop-out.

"What usual reasons?" she asked. In the low light from the lamp, her color seemed high and she looked extremely uncomfortable with the conversation, but still she pressed him for an answer.

"It was inappropriate. I've told myself that a thousand times. I know it was wrong."

"Was it?"

He wished to hell he had some clue what was going through her mind, why she suddenly wanted to chat about this, but she wasn't giving anything away. Did *she* think it was wrong?

"Yes," he finally said, feeling more awkward than he ever remembered. "I put you in an uncomfortable position. I know you're grateful to me for helping with Cameron's rescue. I didn't mean to make you feel indebted to me for that. You're not obligated to me in any way. You're especially not obligated to endure unwelcome, uh, advances. I'm very sorry for that."

She blinked, clearly surprised. "I didn't feel obligated. I don't."

What do you feel? he burned to ask, but he wasn't completely sure he wanted to know the answer. "Good. That's good. I promise, it won't happen again."

He forced a smile, wondering if it looked as ridiculously fake as it felt. "I'm not in the habit of accosting women on the job, I swear."

"You didn't accost me." She pushed around a bit of pasta on her plate, her eyes glued there as if it were the most fascinating corkscrew in the world. "It was only a kiss."

He wouldn't have expected sweet little Megan Vance

to know how to kick a man right in the gonads without even blinking an eye. *Only a kiss.* To him, the world had shifted, the skies had opened, heavenly choirs of angels had burst into song.

To her, it had only been a kiss.

He bared his teeth. "Right. Absolutely."

"I suppose it was just a natural reaction, right? We were both just carried away by emotion, by the sheer, overwhelming relief at finding Cameron after so many hours of intense stress."

"If you say so."

He wasn't quite sure which of them she was trying to convince. He had to admit, he wasn't buying it. He kissed her because he wanted to, more than he wanted to breathe. Because somehow she had made a shambles of the hard, protective shell he used to keep the world out.

Because when he was with her, the world seemed softer, somehow. Sweeter.

"You don't think it was a release of stress?"

He made a rough sound in the back of his throat. "It sure as hell didn't release any of my stress. What about you?"

She blinked at him for a moment, and then she gave a startled laugh. "I suppose it didn't."

After a quick, sidelong look at him, she turned her attention back to the food on her plate. They lapsed into silence and he was racking his tired brain to come up with another subject of conversation when she spoke again, her voice pitched low as if she were revealing some deep, dark secret.

"I can't stop thinking about it," she whispered.

He wasn't sure how he reacted—he hoped to hell he hadn't groaned aloud, though he certainly felt like it.

Still, her emerald gaze flickered to him again, dismay in her eyes.

"I probably shouldn't have said that, should I?"

He cleared his throat. "Depends in what context you're thinking about it—as an experience you found completely repulsive and hope to never have to endure again?"

He paused, his pulse pounding. "Or otherwise?"

She was silent for a long time, the only sound in the little alcove the ticking of a clock on a bookshelf and the pounding of his pulse in his ears. He was an idiot to kiss her and an idiot to care so much about how she had reacted to it.

When she finally spoke, her voice was pitched low, so quiet he could barely hear.

"Otherwise," she whispered.

So much for all the million reasons he told himself he wouldn't kiss her again. Hadn't he just finished telling her it was a mistake and wouldn't happen again?

He stared at her, instantly aroused even though he knew it was insane. How could just a word send heat and hungry need sizzling through him?

"This is crazy, Caleb," she said, her voice ragged and color suddenly climbing her high cheekbones. "We barely know each other. What little time we *have* spent been together has been under the worst conditions imaginable, at least for me."

He took some comfort that she seemed to be desperately trying to convince herself more than him. He knew a decent man would probably try to change the subject to something safe and innocuous, just let the whole thing drop.

He discovered he wasn't very decent after all, at least not when it came to Megan.

"Crazy," he agreed, then he leaned forward and captured her mouth with his.

She sighed his name, her hands fluttered up to twine around his neck and he was lost.

He wanted to devour her like the meal she had just prepared for him, but he ruthlessly beat down the wild need, keeping the kiss soft, easy. She wasn't ready for more. He sensed it as surely as he knew it was killing him to hold back his hunger.

Words of tenderness tangled on his tongue, but he knew she wasn't ready for those, either.

The clock on the bookcase ticked on and as each moment passed, more and more of his control slipped away with it. She was so soft and warm, like slipping aching muscles into a natural hot spring after a hard day of climbing.

"You taste like brownies," she murmured.

You taste like heaven, he wanted to say, but the words caught in his throat when she licked the corner of his mouth.

His control frayed and he deepened the kiss, against his better instincts. Instead of pulling away as he'd feared she would, she let out a breathy little sigh and welcomed him inside her mouth, her hands tangling in his hair. He wanted her like he'd never wanted anything in his life and miraculously, incredibly, she seemed to feel the same thing.

He pulled her onto his lap, desperate to be closer, and she didn't resist. She snuggled closer, pressing her soft curves against him, and he had to wonder if he'd been caught in that cave-in after all and that this just was some delayed version of paradise.

"Mom?"

They both froze, their breathing ragged, as the word drifted down the hallway. She stared at him for perhaps ten seconds, her eyes soft and aroused. Then shock replaced the heat and she scrambled away from him as if he had pinched her.

She opened her mouth to say something, then jerked it shut and hurried down the hall to her son's bedroom, leaving him aching and hungry and wondering what the hell he had just done.

Chapter 14

After she left, Cale sat alone for a few moments, trying to wrestle all his rampaging hormones back under control. He could deal with unsatisfied desire. What he wasn't sure he could handle was this sudden foreboding.

He hadn't missed the expression in Megan's eyes before she had rushed away to deal with her son. She had looked both shocked and dismayed at their heated embrace, and he was fairly certain he had also seen a resigned finality there, like a child reluctantly giving away a toy.

He decided not to worry about what she planned to give up yet. After another moment or two, he rose and joined her in the bedroom.

Cameron was sitting up on the bed, his blond hair messy. He wore X-Men pajamas and looked small and fragile, much like his mother.

He frowned in confusion when Cale walked into the room, head cocked as he no doubt tried to figure out who the strange man in his room might be. After a moment, recognition registered in those eyes that looked so much like his mother's.

"You're the one from the mine. You found me."

He didn't know anything about seizures, but he wouldn't have thought the kid had been alert enough to remember anything that had happened underground. Maybe Cam hadn't been quite as unaware of his surroundings as he had seemed.

He smiled a little. "Right. I'm Caleb Davis."

"Agent Davis is with the FBI," Megan said.

Cameron's eyes widened and he looked at Cale with new interest. "The FBI? Really?"

"He and his partner have been two of the many people looking for you since the morning I realized you were gone."

The intrigue in his eyes shifted quickly to chagrin, and he looked down at his quilt. "I've put everybody to a lot of trouble, haven't I?"

"Yes," Megan said firmly, then moderated her tone. "But everyone is very relieved you're home safe."

Cameron chewed his lip. "I was stupid to get lost. Dad never would have gotten lost or had a dumb seizure."

"Your father made plenty of mistakes." Megan's tone was gentle. "I don't know that he ever decided to explore an abandoned mine by himself, but he took many risks he later admitted hadn't been wise."

"I didn't mean to go so far into the mine. I was just going to go in for a minute. But then I saw…" His voice trailed off and he pulled his knees to his chest, hugging his legs. "I was so scared and I ran and ran and I took a wrong turn and then I didn't know how to find my way back out."

Cale pulled a chair over to the bed. "What happened, Cameron? Why did you run?"

The boy rocked back and forth, his features anxious. Cale hated to push him, but they needed to know so they could take the necessary steps to keep him safe.

His obvious distress must have been too much for his mother. Megan pulled him closer and the boy leaned into her, closing his eyes as if he could block out the nightmare Cale knew he must have endured inside those mine tunnels.

When he spoke, his voice was small and frightened. "I saw something. Something bad."

"What did you see, Cameron?" he pressed.

"I don't want to say."

Megan now looked as distressed as her son. If he could spare her this, he would have. But through years of experience interviewing crime witnesses, he knew Cameron would feel better only after he had talked about what he had seen and shared the burden of it.

Cale drew the chair closer to the bed and gave the boy a reassuring look. "I think I know what you saw, Cameron. We found someone else in that mine besides you. Someone who had been shot and killed. Did you see that happen?"

A shudder shook his small frame. He didn't say anything, just shook his head. "I didn't see, but I heard it."

Megan pulled him closer, her delicate features pale in the low light of the room.

"I saw lights on the mountain going into the mine," Cameron said. "I thought they were terrorists making a bomb and I thought they must be using the mine tunnels. I sneaked inside to see what they were doing. I know it was wrong, but I was pretending I was like my dad. He was a hero and I wanted to be one, too. I wanted to catch the bad guys. But when I went inside, it smelled funny. Different from the times I went in before, and I didn't like it. Then I heard them."

Cale's heart clenched when he thought of the danger the boy had put himself in. As traumatic as his ordeal must have been inside the mine, Cale knew it could have been much, much worse if he had been caught by the meth cook or his killer.

"How many people did you hear?"

"Two men."

"Could you see their faces?"

"It was too dark and I didn't want them to see me so I didn't go closer. But I could tell they weren't terrorists. They were yelling and fighting. About money, I think, but I couldn't really tell."

"What did they say?"

"The one who sounded familiar was talking about cooking and his aunt Mabel and bags with nickels."

"You recognized one voice?"

Cameron hesitated. "I don't know. I thought it sounded like someone I had heard before. Someone I knew from somewhere, but I couldn't tell for sure where or how I knew him."

"Was he young or old?"

"I don't know. He just sounded mean, I guess."

His voice trailed off and he shivered again. Megan sent Cale a pleading look, begging him silently to stop.

He didn't want to upset her or her son further, but he knew he had no choice.

"What happened after that, Cam?"

The boy's chin wobbled. "It's like you said. They were fighting and then the other one sounded scared and said he was just joking around and the first one said he didn't have a sense of humor."

He screwed up his face as if he could block the memories out. "And then I heard two loud bangs and I knew he shot him, like on TV. I was afraid he would shoot me, so I ran. I went into a tunnel I hadn't been in before just to hide for a while. I was just going to wait until he was gone and then find my way back out, but I...I got turned around and couldn't find the way out. I looked and looked and looked but I was just going deeper and deeper, until I didn't know where I was."

He swiped at a tear. "I was just a big baby. I shouldn't have been so scared. Dad wouldn't have been so scared or so dumb."

Cale couldn't help himself. He leaned closer, looking intently into the boy's brimming eyes. "Listen to me, Cameron. You are not dumb. You were smart enough to get away from a dangerous situation and you were smart enough to survive in there on your own and to leave marks so you could backtrack the way you had come. That's the only reason we found you, Cam. Because you pointed the way for us."

The boy looked as if he desperately wanted to believe him. "You really think so?"

"Absolutely. You shouldn't have gone in there in the first place—you know that now, right?"

Cameron nodded.

"And when you realized you were lost, you should have stayed put so rescuers could find you, instead of going farther and farther into the mine tunnels. You made some mistakes, but you did a lot of things right. I don't know a lot of grown men who could have survived what you did in there, Cameron."

The boy looked desperate to believe him. His eyes searched Cale's. After a moment, he gave a hesitant smile. "I was really scared," he admitted. "Especially after I used up all the flashlight batteries."

"I don't blame you one bit," Cale answered. "I was scared going in there, too, and I had a field telephone and plenty of light and somebody with me the whole time."

He didn't add that he was mostly scared he would have to bring Megan back her son's body. The boy didn't need to know that.

"You're not going to ever do anything like that again, are you?" Megan said sternly.

Cameron shook his head hard. "No way. I swear."

"The sheriff is going to want to talk to you," Cale said after a moment. "I can tell him what you told me, but I'm sure he'll want to hear it for himself. He'll probably have more questions for you. Do you think you can work on trying to figure out why that voice sounded familiar?"

The boy's eyes turned grim. "I don't like to think about it."

"I know it's scary and hard. But if you can give us even a couple of ideas, that would be a big help in finding the bad guy. You can be a hero after all, just like your dad."

"I'll try." He paused. "Uh, thanks for finding me and stuff."

"You're welcome." Cale smiled at the boy, then

risked a glance at his mother. Megan was looking at him with a soft expression he couldn't quite read. Before he could puzzle it out, Cameron spoke again.

"Can I have something to eat? I'm really hungry."

"Of course!" Megan said instantly. "I've got your favorite sandwich already made. PB & J. How about a big glass of milk to go with it?"

"Oh, yeah!" Cameron said.

"I'll go downstairs for some milk while you bring in the sandwich," Cale offered.

When he returned with the milk, he found Megan on the landing at the top of the stairs, clearing up the remains of their shared meal that had ended with such disastrous heat.

Her gaze shot quickly to his, then she turned her attention back to the plates in her hand. He knew her sudden nervousness around him had more to do with their kiss than his questioning of Cameron. But since he wasn't at all ready to discuss the former, he chose to focus on the latter.

"I'm sorry I had to push Cam about what he witnessed inside the mine," he said. "I could tell it upset you."

"You only did what you had to. He was going to have to talk about it sooner or later." She frowned. "Do you really think the killer might be someone he knows? Someone from Moose Springs?"

"It makes sense. Somebody knew enough about this area to find that mine entrance so they could use it for a meth lab. And the murder victim is local. It's logical he would be working with someone from around here."

"I can't imagine who it might be, if indeed it's someone

familiar. Cameron hasn't met many people at all. We've only been here a few months! I can probably name on one hand the adult males he's met besides his uncle—his new soccer coach, the pastor at church, the elementary school principal. See, I can't even come up with five names. How could anyone we know be a murderer?"

In her agitation, she nearly dropped the whole tray on the floor. He took it from her. He was loath to worry her further, but knew she needed to face reality, however grim it might be.

"Megan, if the guy *is* from around here, he has to know about Cameron's disappearance and his rescue from the mine. It won't take him long to figure out Cam probably saw something."

"I know," she said in a small voice. "It's not over, is it?"

He longed to pull her into his arms but sensed she wouldn't welcome it.

"Not yet. But with Cameron's help, it soon will be."

"Will you keep him safe?"

He gazed at her, unable to resist the plea in her green eyes. She could ask him to move that mountain out there and he knew he would go find a bulldozer and start digging.

"I'll do my best," he said gruffly.

It was a promise he prayed he could keep.

"No frigging way. Are you crazy?" Cale snapped at the sheriff several hours later.

Late morning sunlight streamed in through the kitchen window, sending shafts of light across the table. From here, Megan watched Cameron and Hailey playing Go Fish on the coffee table in the great room. She could hear Hailey's sweet giggle at something her brother said and see a sunbeam gleaming white in Cam's hair.

After the trauma of the last few days, this would have been a perfect moment—except for the two hard, dangerous men glowering at each other over coffee.

Though he looked annoyed, Daniel Galvez didn't rise to the bait, and she thought again how much she had come to appreciate his unruffled demeanor in just about every situation.

"I didn't say I was in favor of the idea. I'm only presenting it to Megan, who ultimately must make the final decision."

She squirmed as they both turned their attention to her. She wanted to hug her children close and enjoy the beauty of a Saturday morning in August, not become embroiled in their disagreement.

"You didn't say you opposed the idea, either," she pointed out to the sheriff. "I would like to know your true opinion before I make any kind of decision."

The subject of Cale's wrath seemed innocuous enough. Every year Moose Springs threw a big celebration, Moosemania Days, complete with a parade, a carnival on the town square, a barbecue thrown by the Rotary Club and a fireworks display.

The celebration had been put on hold during the search for Cameron. Since his rescue, the town was apparently ready to party and the mayor had approached Daniel about having Cameron be the guest of honor at the barbecue that evening.

The sheriff sighed. "I can't answer that, Megan. You're going to have to make the decision. I *can* tell you, there is a town full of people who spent a lot of time and energy looking for Cam. I doubt there was a family in Moose Springs that wasn't involved somehow in the search. Those who weren't out there actively volunteering were at home baking for the searchers—and praying for Cameron's safe return. This entire town came out to look for him. They want to share in your happiness that he's been found."

"So you think I should take him?"

"You know, he doesn't have to be there for the town to celebrate his return. But having him show up even for a few moments would mean a lot to the people who took time out of their lives to look for him."

"Sure," Cale said, a sharp bite to his voice. "Especially to the bastard who killed a nineteen-year-old kid over a meth deal."

She winced at his bluntness, even though she knew he was right. She hadn't forgotten there was a murderer still out there, someone who could have Cameron in his sights right now.

On the other hand, she couldn't discount what Daniel had said. She and her family had been the recipients of a huge outpouring of support and help while Cam had been missing.

Most people in Moose Springs didn't even know her. She was a newcomer, a stranger to most, yet they hadn't hesitated, had responded in force when she and her family needed help.

She supposed she could always go in Cameron's place to express her gratitude, but she knew people wanted to see her son. If he showed up to say thank-you, even for a moment, perhaps they would feel validated for all their hard work and perhaps know some small degree of her deep and eternal gratitude.

"Can you protect him?" she asked Daniel.

"Yes."

"Not completely," Cale argued.

"There will be four hundred people there with their eyes trained on Cameron every moment," the sheriff answered. "What do you really think is going to happen in the middle of a town celebration?"

"Who knows?" Caleb said. "I sure as hell don't want to find out."

"Remind me again why you're still here," Daniel said in that slow, laconic tone of his. "I was under the impression from Agent McKinnon that the FBI was no longer involved in this case."

Cale snapped his mouth shut and Megan stared down at her hands. She had a good idea why he hadn't left. He felt personally responsible for Cameron, especially after she had begged him the night before to protect her son.

To her relief, Daniel didn't wait for an answer to his question. "It's not your decision anyway," he said again. "It's Megan's."

They both looked at her again and she sighed. She didn't want to take Cameron anywhere. She wanted to keep him home forever and wrap him in cotton batting. But she owed it to the people of this town who had given so much of themselves.

"All right," she said quickly, before she could change her mind. "Tell the mayor we'll be there."

The sheriff nodded. "Everyone who spent time looking for him has a vested interest in keeping him safe. You can be sure we won't let anything happen to him."

His radio squawked suddenly and a dispatcher broke in to tell him he was needed to break up a dispute between carnival workers. The sheriff rose, and she wondered if the man ever slept.

"I can send a car to pick you up at six," he said.

"That won't be necessary," she answered, then showed him to the front door.

When she returned to the kitchen, she found Cale still looking tired and out of sorts, but so gorgeous it was all she could do to keep her hands firmly in her pockets.

"You think I made the wrong decision?" she asked him.

He didn't answer her question. "I'm coming with you," he said instead, giving her no room to argue, even if she had wanted to.

"I was hoping you would say that," she admitted. "I'll feel much better about this if I know you're there watching out for Cam."

Their gazes held for a charged moment, and in his eyes she saw all the heat and hungry need she had run from in such a panic the night before.

A muscle worked in his jaw and he was the first one to look away. "Daniel's right," he said. "This is no longer an FBI concern, since there has been no overt threat to Cameron. Gage packed it up yesterday and I'm going to have to join him soon."

She nodded, trying hard to ignore the pain stabbing her heart. "I expected as much."

"I don't want to leave until this guy is caught, but I don't have a choice here. A case we've been working on for several months is coming to a head and it looks like we'll be making some major busts next week."

Will it be dangerous? she wondered, then chided herself for even wasting time forming the question. Of course it would be dangerous. He was an FBI agent who arrested hardened criminals.

That muscle flexed in his jaw again and she wondered why he seemed so ill at ease. "You know I have friends here," he said after a moment. "Mason and Jane Keller."

She had met the rancher and his lovely British wife before and liked both them and their two children. She had no idea how Cale could have met them, but this didn't seem the right time to ask.

She also couldn't quite figure out why he was telling her about his friendship with the Kellers until he reached across the table and captured her hand in his, the first time he had touched her since the night before. She wasn't prepared for the instant electric charge between them, or the way his larger hand seemed to engulf hers.

"I come to Moose Springs often on my way to the Bittercreek. I would like to see you again under happier circumstances."

She stared at him, totally unprepared for this.

"Why?" she asked, then flushed. Had she really asked such a stupid question?

His fingers wrapped around hers and she couldn't help the shiver at his touch.

His sharp-eyed gaze didn't miss it. "That's why," he said quietly. "There's something between us, Megan— something I didn't expect and certainly wasn't looking for, but it's there. I...care about you. I'm not sure how it happened, especially under these difficult circumstances, but you've become very important to me. You and your children."

A sweet warmth fluttered through her. She wanted to sit in this sun-dappled kitchen and soak up his words, to pull him toward her and let his strength surround her.

Her hand clenched and his fingers curled around them—the fingers that were connected to an arm that was connected to a shoulder with a bullet hole in it.

At the stark reminder, the joy blooming inside her turned instantly black and frost-singed.

She slid her hand away from under his and folded it tightly on her lap, pressing it to her stomach. "I'm sure whatever it is is only a byproduct of the…the intensity of the situation."

"Maybe. That's not all there is to it, though. I've been involved in hundreds of cases during my years at the FBI. Some that have ripped my guts out, and some that have consumed me for months. No one I've met in any of those cases has ever reached inside me like you have."

Megan took a shaky breath, feeling light-headed and almost nauseous. She wasn't ready for this. She *wasn't*.

She had tried to tell herself she had been imagining things the night before, had read far too much into a few little kisses. She surely couldn't possibly be falling in love with this hard, dangerous man. It was impossible. Utterly impossible.

She couldn't let herself. That was all there was to it. She had lost too much in her life. Her parents, her brother. Rick.

She couldn't survive loving and losing Cale.

Her resolve wavered at the emotion in those blue eyes. How could she ever have thought them cool and distant in those early hours of the investigation? Now those eyes seemed to shimmer with heat, with banked emotion.

She closed her own eyes, hating this. Her heart already felt as if it would crack apart, but she knew this was only a small spasm of pain compared to what would be in store for her if she didn't do her best to repair the holes he had battered in her defenses.

Unable to face him, she drew in a shuddering breath, her gaze glued to the pattern on the tablecloth. "I don't think that would be a very good idea," she finally said, her voice low. "Seeing you again, I mean."

He said nothing for several beats. "No?"

Her gaze flashed to his, then down at the tablecloth once more. "I'm grateful to you for what you've done. More grateful than I can begin to tell you."

Her fingers trembled on her lap. She had to hope the table hid them from his probing gaze so he wouldn't guess she was lying, trying to come up with any excuse to push him away.

"I could try to pretend those feelings of gratitude are something else, to make them more than they are. For a while, I might even succeed in convincing both of us. But gratitude would only take me so far."

"You never know. Something more might develop."

"It wouldn't. I wouldn't let it."

He blinked at her bluntness, and she saw hurt in those blue depths before he quickly concealed it. "Oh?"

She pressed a fist to her stomach, sick at herself. She couldn't do this. She couldn't make him think she was coolly indifferent to him, not after everything he had done for her. It was cruel and cowardly.

She sighed. "I owe you so much for what you have done for me and my family."

"Forget about that for a moment," he said sharply.

"I can't. I owe you everything, which means I owe you at least the truth, no matter how painful it is for both of us."

Her gaze flashed to his, then she looked down at her coffee mug, one Rick had helped Cameron buy for her out of his allowance the last Mother's Day before he died.

"I barely survived losing my husband," she whispered. "I didn't eat or sleep for weeks and I thought I was dying, too. I think I would have, if not for the children. The worst part was that while his death was hard enough, in many ways, living with him was even harder. I hated his job. I hated the risks he took, hated knowing every day might be the day the Navy chaplain showed up at my door."

"Megan—"

"I can't go through that again. I'm not strong enough. If I were ever to consider a…a relationship with someone, he would have to be someone safe. He could never be a soldier or a firefighter or a police officer." She paused. "Or an FBI agent who's already been shot at least once on the job and who caves and rock climbs on the side."

He said nothing for a long moment. When she finally risked a look at him, she saw the bleakness had returned to his expression. "I guess that's clear enough," he murmured.

"I'm sorry." It seemed grossly inadequate, but she knew there was nothing else she could say.

"Don't be. I appreciate your honesty." He smiled slightly, but she saw the shadows had returned in his eyes.

After a pause, he changed the subject. "I'll talk to the sheriff tonight at the celebration to make sure he puts measures in place to protect you and Cameron after I'm gone."

"Thank you," she murmured, fighting down her misery.

Hailey ran in before he could say anything in response.

"Mommy, can you come play with us?" she begged.

"Of course, sweetheart," she answered, seizing the chance to escape the thick, awkward tension.

She was aware of him sitting at the table with his coffee while she shuffled the deck and dealt the cards. After a few moments, he rose and she heard the door leading to the deck open and close as he walked outside into the August morning.

She held her cards tightly, fighting tears and despising herself for being such a craven coward.

Chapter 15

He had to admit, this was all pretty cool.

Maybe a Navy SEAL would think it was lame and boring, but Cameron wasn't a SEAL. It had been fun to pretend for a while, until he had been so stupid and took the make-believe too far. But sometimes it was more fun being nine years old, especially when people were being so nice to him.

A big sign over the bower in the park read Welcome Home, Cameron, just as if he were some kind of returning war hero. There had to be like a jillion people here. Most of them he didn't know, but they all acted super happy to see him.

It made him feel kind of bad about how rotten he'd been to his mom when she told him they were moving away from San Diego and all his friends and his dad's SEAL team. He had been a big baby about it, telling her he didn't want to move to some hick town in Utah, even if they would be closer to his cousins and his aunt and uncle.

Because he had been mad about moving here, he had been pretty mean about it for a while. But he was starting to think maybe he'd been wrong about Moose Springs. People here were treating him like some kind of movie star.

"There's my boy." He looked up to find his aunt Molly next to him. She opened her arms and pulled him into a big hug. Every time she had seen him today, she had hugged him tight as if she couldn't get enough. Usually he would have tried to get away as fast as he could, but since his rescue, he decided he didn't mind.

She smelled like chocolate-chip cookies, and his stomach grumbled. When were they going to stop all this yakking and get to the food? he wondered. He had been eating all day long but he was still hungry. Everything tasted so good to him, maybe because he had to spend those two days in the mine only eating a couple of lousy granola bars.

His uncle Scott wasn't far behind Aunt Molly. He didn't hug Cam, thank goodness, he just put a hand on his shoulder and smiled down at him.

"It sure is good to see you, kid," he said, and Cam got a funny lump in his throat.

He liked his uncle a lot. He didn't do exciting stuff like blow up things and parachute behind enemy lines like his dad had done before he died.

But he was never too busy to kick a soccer ball in the backyard with Nate and Cam, and he even sometimes played Barbies with McKenna and Hailey, which Cam thought was weird but kind of nice.

Somebody called out to his uncle. He gave Cam another squeeze on the shoulder, then turned away to talk to whoever it was.

It was fun to have everyone be so nice to him, but he was getting pretty tired of standing around with all the grown-ups. He looked on the edge of the bowery and saw Hailey playing in the grass with Kenna and some other kids he didn't know.

He wanted to be there with them—even more, he wanted to go on the Vomit Comet with his cousin Nate as they had talked about. But his mom said he had to stand here in this dumb shirt and tie and be nice to all the people who had helped look for him.

What were the chances Mom would let him go after they ate dinner? He had been here like forever. She would probably say no—she was funny about some things like that—but he decided he had to ask. He didn't want to miss his chance. Really, how often did the carnival come to Moose Springs?

He turned to ask her about it, but some lady was talking to his mom and he knew he would have to wait until they were done or Mom would get mad at him for interrupting the grown-ups.

His gaze wandered around the crowd while he waited and he caught sight of Agent Davis, the guy who had found him and pulled him out of the mine.

He liked the FBI agent. They had spent a lot of time together that day. He knew a ton about climbing and had asked Cameron to show him his escape route out the window.

He wanted to know all about it, how Cam had spent a week making the finger holes with his dad's hand drill when his mom wasn't looking and how he had practiced and practiced until he could go up and down fast.

Cameron didn't think the FBI agent had really believed he could do it until he showed him. The look of shocked amazement in his eyes had been pretty cool.

Of course, Agent Davis made him swear he wouldn't ever use them again. Then Mom said he could swear up and down all he wanted, but she was still going to find somebody to fill in the holes.

He thought about asking Agent Davis if *he* wanted to go on the Vomit Comet, too, but when he looked at him again, the words clogged in his throat, like the time he ate too big a bite of hot dog. The FBI agent was staring at Cam's mom with a really weird look on his face, a look that made Cam's stomach feel funny.

Agent Davis looked at his mom for a long time, then tilted his head down and found Cameron watching him. The weird look disappeared, and he kind of smiled at Cameron. Even though he didn't feel like it and even though he didn't want to think about what that look might be all about, he made himself smile back.

The lady talking to his mom finally moved away but before Cam could talk to her about the ride, somebody else came up to his mom, a skinny guy with a mustache he thought might be one of his mom's tax clients.

The guy hugged her. "This is a much happier day than the last time I saw you," he said in a laughing kind of voice.

When he heard it, Cam froze and suddenly he couldn't breathe. His face felt hot and cold at the same time. He was afraid it might be one of those aura-thingies his neuro doctor talked about, that he might be heading for another stupid seizure.

No. That wasn't it. He knew why he felt sick. Wild panic burst through him and he wanted to run away and hide, especially when the guy turned to him.

"There's the young man of the hour," he said, and Cameron was afraid he was going to puke.

He knew that voice!

The last time he heard it had been in the mine, right before he heard gunshots.

This had to rank right up there as just about the most miserable, god-awful evening of his life.

Cale stood on the edge of the bowery, doing his best to keep his expression impassive, emotionless, as he scanned the crowd for any possible threat.

Despite his efforts to focus only on keeping Cameron safe, he couldn't seem to prevent these random moments of deep, painful yearning.

His chest felt tight and achy as he watched Megan accept hugs and good wishes from the people of Moose Springs. She was so lovely and serene, glowing from the inside out with her relief at having her son safe. He couldn't help wondering how the hell he was going to go on without her for the rest of his life.

He was staring. He knew he was, but he couldn't seem to look away. He suddenly felt someone's gaze on him and found Cam watching *him* watch Megan.

From somewhere deep inside, Caleb mustered a casual smile for the boy. After a moment, Cameron returned it hesitantly, then turned back to the woman talking to his mother.

When he left tonight and returned to Salt Lake City and the rest of his life, he would be leaving a jagged chunk of his heart here in this little town. Not all of it belonged to Megan, either. Somehow during the search—even before he found the boy—he had come to care about Cameron and Hailey, as well.

His life would seem colorless and drab without all of them.

"Agent Davis," a female voice said loudly into his ear. He turned away to find Megan's sister, Molly Randall, standing next to him, a strange light in her eyes. He had the uncomfortable feeling she had been trying to get his attention for some time.

"Yes?" he asked, hoping like hell his emotions weren't plastered all over his face for everyone to see.

She blinked a little at his abrupt tone. "Um, Meg tells me you're leaving after the party. I wanted to tell you again before you go how obliged we all are for what you've done."

He shifted, uneasy with her gratitude. Word must have spread about the details of Cameron's rescue and the tunnel collapse they had narrowly missed. All evening, he had been doing his best to fend off praise and effusive thanks from the people of Moose Springs.

It made him itchy and out of sorts because he didn't know how to respond. He wasn't any good at accepting gratitude, and he knew he wasn't some kind of hero.

He had been doing a job, that's all. The real heroes were the hundreds of volunteer searchers who had given up sleep and food and time with their families to look for the boy.

Cale and Ben Lucero just happened to have been the first ones lucky enough to stumble across him.

He forced his features into what he hoped was a

polite smile at Megan's sister. "I'm glad I could be in the right place at the right time."

To his further discomfort, she took his hands in hers and squeezed them. "It was more than that, and everyone knows it. I heard the details of the rescue from the sheriff. I know you risked your own life to pull Cameron out of that cave and that you reinjured yourself in the process. We can never repay you for returning him to us."

She reached up on tiptoe and kissed him on the cheek. "I just wanted you to know you always have friends in Moose Springs. No matter what, you're always welcome."

Not everywhere. Megan had made no secret that she didn't want him here anymore after tonight. She wanted him to go back to Salt Lake City and take his inconvenient feelings with him. He wondered if Molly Randall would continue to look at him with such open friendliness if she knew her sister had pushed him away.

"Thank you," he murmured, trying to fight down the hollow ache in his chest.

Above Molly's head, his gaze strayed to Megan, as it tended to do whenever possible. He was just in time to catch sight of a lean man with carefully styled blond hair and a mustache hugging her. He had seen the guy around the search command center, he remembered, and had thought then that he looked entirely too smoothly manicured to be of much use on a rough-and-ready SAR unit.

What was their relationship? he wondered as the man continued to hug her a moment longer than necessary. Jealousy spurted through him, taking him completely off guard.

He had no right to be jealous of anything having to

do with Megan Vance, he reminded himself sternly. She had told him so with unavoidable certainty.

Still, something about the other man raised Cale's hackles. Was this the kind of man she wanted? Someone smooth and polished and soft?

Something was off. He couldn't put a finger on it, but his instincts were suddenly humming and it wasn't just from the man's apparent familiarity with Megan.

His gaze shifted to Cameron and those humming instincts shoved him like a fist in the solar plexus. Something was definitely wrong. The boy's features had lost every bit of color, and he looked as if he was going to lose the vast quantities of food he'd been putting away all day.

Cale didn't take time to think through his actions. He just crossed the short distance between them and took up position behind the boy, his hand casually set in easy reach of his weapon.

Megan gave him a startled look at his protective stance, then cleared her throat. "Uh, Cale, this is one of the clients of my accounting business, Wayne Shumway. Wayne is on the Moose Springs Search and Rescue team. Wayne, this is Caleb Davis."

Something flashed in the man's gaze, but it was gone so quickly Cale couldn't figure it out. He smiled a little too broadly. "You're the FBI agent who found Cam in the mine, right?"

He could feel the boy shudder and knew he was clinging to his fraying control. "That's right," he said, his mind racing to come up with some excuse to separate the boy from the crowd so he could find out what was wrong, though his gut had already guessed it.

"I've never been involved in an underground rescue,"

Shumway said, "though I did help bring a couple stranded hikers down from the face of Mount Baldy. Let me tell you, that was quite an experience."

The man settled in for what was probably a long story, no doubt painting himself in the brightest light possible, but Cale cut him off before he could even begin.

"I'd love to hear that story. Maybe we can grab a beer later and you can tell me all about it. But right now, we're on our way to grab a burger. Will you excuse us?"

He grabbed hold of Megan's arm with one hand and slung the other across Cam's shoulders.

Megan blinked at him, clearly baffled by his insistence. "But I don't…" Her voice broke off when he squeezed her arm hard.

He wanted to kiss her right there in front of everyone when she nodded after only the slightest pause.

"Right. A burger. I'm starving." She manufactured a polite smile. "Excuse us, Wayne, won't you? And thank you again for all your help during the search."

Shumway nodded. "Sure. Of course."

He leaned down and smiled at Cameron, but Cale didn't miss the sudden hardness in his light blue eyes. "I'm sure glad you're not still stuck in that mine, son."

With his arm around the boy's shoulders protectively, Cale could feel a shudder rack his thin frame and he knew he needed to get Cameron out of there *now*.

"We all are," he said, then tugged them both toward the area of the park where the Rotary Club had set up several large half-barrel barbecues.

A small band stage was set up for a performance later, but it was blessedly quiet now. He took them behind it, out of sight in case Shumway was watching.

"Caleb, what is going on?" Megan asked when they were some distance away. "I don't want a hamburger."

He didn't answer, only crouched down so he could be on the boy's level. "Cameron?"

The boy had lost none of that panicky look. His green-eyed gaze met Cale's, and they shared an unspoken communication. He nodded. "That was the man I heard."

He had suspected it by the boy's instinctive reaction, but hearing it still sent rage coursing through him. Because of that slick-looking bastard, Cameron and Megan had lived through two days of hell; right then, he wanted to rip him apart with his bare hands.

"Wayne Shumway?" Megan's features reflected her shock. "That's impossible! He's...he's a respected community leader. He owns three businesses in town—the service station, an auto repair business and a sandwich franchise! They're all very successful. I should know. I'm his accountant! Why would he need to deal drugs?"

Instead of answering, he looked squarely at the boy. "Cameron, are you positive?"

He nodded. "I couldn't forget that voice. That must be why I thought I knew him, because I must have answered the phone before when he called to talk to my mom."

Cale squeezed his shoulder. "If you say it's him, that's all that matters to me."

Megan looked shaken, and he could see her trying to put away her shock for her son's sake. "You're right. Of course you're right. I don't understand it, but if you believe that's the man you heard, then it must be."

She turned to Cale, looking at him with a trust that humbled him. "What do we do now?"

"We need to find Daniel first."

"I saw him over by the swings when you dragged us over here," she said. She looked as pale as Cameron now, her green eyes huge in her delicate features.

Though he wanted to pull her into his arms and promise her everything would be all right, he knew he couldn't. Even if things between them weren't so tense and awkward, this wasn't the time.

For now, he needed to focus all his energies on keeping them safe.

The next half hour was a blur of shock and worry for Megan.

It was surreal, really, that they could be having this conversation in the middle of a town celebration while children ran past with cotton candy and a baseball game went on just a few yards away.

One part of her still had a hard time fathoming that one of her best clients—a man she had welcomed into her home and had worked with alone on numerous occasions—could be capable of dealing drugs and, worse, cold-blooded murder.

At the same time, she couldn't doubt Cameron's un-shakable conviction. Her son was absolutely convinced Wayne was the man he heard commit a terrible murder inside the mine and she believed him. Cam wouldn't lie or make up stories, not about something this important.

What would she have done without Caleb there? She didn't want to guess. She knew it was completely unfair of her to push him away with brusque decisiveness one moment and to lean on him for support and counsel the next, but she was deeply grateful for the way he had instantly taken charge of the situation.

He should be washing his hands of them, not conferring with Daniel Galvez about the next step they needed to take. But she couldn't deny the comfort she found in his presence.

When they found the sheriff and told him Cameron had identified the man he heard inside the mine as Wayne, the sheriff had reacted with the same shock she had.

To her vast relief, after that first moment of disbelief, he had been willing to trust Cameron's convictions, though he had also faced the situation with his typical pragmatism.

"I wish I could give you a better answer, but we can't arrest Shumway just on the word of a nine-year-old boy," he said now. "We're going to have to build a case against him and that's going to take some time, I'm afraid."

"In the meantime, what measures can you take to protect Cameron and his family until he is arrested?" Cale asked.

"Protect us?" Megan asked in disbelief. "Do you really think we're in some kind of danger from…from *Wayne?*"

"He's already killed once," Caleb said flatly. "He couldn't have missed Cameron's frightened reaction to him tonight. By now, he's probably putting the pieces together and figuring out Cam knows something. It's not too great a stretch to anticipate him doing whatever is necessary to keep the boy quiet."

This was a nightmare, one that just seemed to drag on and on.

"You know the limitations of my small department," Daniel said. "I just don't have the staff for round-the-clock surveillance. Do you have any suggestions?"

Cale's mouth tightened with frustration, and she saw

the wheels turning as he tried to come up with a solution. "How much time do you think you're going to need?"

"I can't answer that. I would guess at least a few days."

"They can come stay with me in Salt Lake City," Cale said, his tone abrupt and decisive.

Megan stared at him. "What?"

"I've got a house on the Avenues with two spare bedrooms and a big backyard for the kids. Shumway will never think to look for you there. After he's in custody, it should be safe to return home."

"Perfect." Daniel looked relieved, a sentiment Megan absolutely did *not* share.

"Don't I get any say in this?" She glared at both men.

Daniel shifted, discomfort plain on his handsome features. "This is the best alternative for you and the kids, Megan."

Best for whom? Certainly not her. She needed to put distance between them, not move in with the man, for heaven's sake!

Cale seemed to sense the source of her unease. "Like Daniel said, it will probably only be for a few days and I'll be working most of that time. You likely won't even see me."

This was supposed to make her feel better, that he was going to dump her at his house and she would have to sit by and watch him go out and save the world?

"We'll check into a hotel," she said firmly.

Both men looked as if they wanted to argue but she shook her head. "We'll be fine. It will be like a vacation for the children. A chance for us to spend some time together before school starts in a few weeks."

"We can work out those details on the way to Salt

Lake," Cale said, his features hard and unyielding. He had no intention of allowing her to stay in a hotel. She could see it in the implacable set of his jaw and the determination in his eyes.

She wanted to argue with him, to remind him he had no authority over her. But she could say nothing with the sheriff looking on.

"All right," she finally said. "I'm going to need to go back to the house to pack some things first. Cameron's medication, some clothes, a few toys."

He looked as if he wanted to balk at even that, but he finally nodded tersely.

"Fine, but we'll have to move fast."

Chapter 16

He didn't like this. Not one damn bit. From the passenger seat of Megan's SUV, Cale checked the rearview mirror for any sign of a tail. He couldn't see anything as she pulled away from the city park and into light traffic.

She drove like she did just about everything, he was learning—with competence and control.

Her house was some distance from the town center, and theirs was soon the only vehicle on the road as the houses thinned. A few news teams had lingered in town after Cameron's rescue to do follow-up features, but now they must all have been at the city park videotaping the celebration. The rural road leading to her house was deserted.

"She's down for the count," Megan said when they were close to her house, gesturing to the backseat.

He looked behind her to find Hailey curled up in the corner, her cheek pressed against the leather seat and a lock of red hair slipping out of her braid to curve across her face.

He sighed, wondering when he had last slept with such carefree abandon. Had he ever?

Cameron, on the other hand, sat rigid and tense, his jaw clamped tightly and his hand gripping the armrest on the door as if he feared he would need to bolt from the vehicle at any second.

No child should have to bear such a burden, he thought, aching for the boy. He had escaped one nightmare only to be hurled straight into another one.

"Everything's going to be okay, Cameron," he said, compelled to ease his nervousness. "I'll watch out for you and your mom and sister. I won't let anything happen to you all, I swear it."

Though he could only pray it was a promise within his ability to keep, the boy seemed to take comfort. His tight grip eased on the door and the tight set of his shoulders relaxed a little.

"I can help if I have to. Shredder and Lieutenant Jamison and the guys taught me how to shoot a gun back in San Diego."

Megan drew in a quick breath, her gaze jerking to the rearview mirror. "Cameron! Why didn't you tell me?"

He shrugged. "The guys in the unit said you might not like it. But I begged them, so they finally did. I told them I had to learn how to protect you and Hailey since Dad was dead and you didn't have anyone else to watch out for you. Except now we have Agent Davis, I guess."

Now Megan's glance shifted to him, and Cale saw

slight color bloom across her cheekbones. It lasted only a moment before she turned back to her son.

"I don't like you keeping things from me, Cam."

"I'm sorry," he said in a small voice. "I wanted to know how, just in case."

"I don't think there will be any need for you to fire any weapons," Cale assured him. "Everything's going to be fine. We'll gather some of your things and find a nice place for you guys to hang out for a few days, just until we can clear this up."

"I just wanted you to know I can use a gun if I have to."

"I'll keep that in mind," he said as Megan pulled into her driveway.

The sun was setting over the mountains and in the twilight her house looked serene and welcoming, its logs a warm honey-gold in the fading light.

All looked in order but every instinct still warned him to be cautious. If the man guessed Cameron could identify him, Shumway would panic. Cale had too much experience with cornered rats, and he knew a desperate one might take chances he wouldn't otherwise consider.

He scanned the exterior of the house and the gardens, wishing he'd had the foresight to ask Daniel to send a deputy along with them. He needed to clear the house, but he hated leaving them unprotected and alone out here, even for a moment.

"I want you to wait here in the car while I go inside and check things out," he told Megan in a low, calm voice, hoping Cameron didn't hear and overreact.

"Once I make sure the house is clear, I'll come back out and sit with Hailey and Cameron while you pack what you need."

"All right," she said, pulling the keys out of the ignition. "Here's the house key. It's the square one. The security code is 0-6-3-3."

He could see she still wasn't convinced of the danger, but he didn't want to go into all the reasons for his caution, not with Cameron watching them with that lingering fear in his eyes. The boy trusted him to keep them safe, and Cale planned to do his damnedest.

"Lock the doors," he said.

Once out of the car, he waited until he heard her engage the locks, then worked the snap on the holster concealed at the small of his back. He couldn't have put a finger on the source of his edginess, but he had enough experience in the field not to question it. When his instincts told him to be careful, he listened.

It was a lesson he had learned well, one that had saved his life several times—most recently from Andy Decker's psychotic breakdown and subsequent ambush.

He unlocked the door, then punched in the code on the console in the entry. He flipped on the lights and did a quick sweep of the house, going from room to room. All seemed quiet, but he still couldn't shake the uneasiness dogging him.

He would just have to wake Hailey up and bring both children inside while Megan gathered what they needed for the next few days, he decided. He didn't want her in the house by herself.

He gave one more look around, then opened the front door when suddenly a scream pierced the twilight.

His heart gave one hard thud of panic, then he reached for his weapon and raced onto the porch. To his horror, he found a dark shape pounding on the locked

doors of the SUV. Cale caught a quick look at the terrified faces of Megan and the children.

It had to be Shumway. The bastard must have hiked
in, since he couldn't see any other vehicle.

"FBI! Freeze!" he yelled, fury and fear a tangled
knot inside him. Instead of complying, Shumway
turned, his face wild with panic. Cale saw the gun in his
hand at the same instant he heard a loud pop and felt
agonizing fire explode in his thigh.

He crumpled to the porch floor but was able to keep
hold of his weapon even as waves of pain roared through
him. He squeezed off one shot but it hit the SUV with
a metallic thud. He heard more screams from inside.

Son of a *bitch*. He couldn't fire on the bastard without
running the risk of shattering a window and hitting
someone inside.

He blocked out the pain and crawled on his belly for
cover around the corner of the porch as Shumway continued firing with panicked abandon.

Any minute now, Shumway was going to turn to the
SUV and start firing inside. Just the possibility turned
Cale's blood to ice. Cale knew he didn't have much time.

Come on, Megan. Drive away, he prayed, then he remembered he had used her keys to get into the house.
They were a heavy weight in his pocket.

She could do nothing but sit there in the middle of
the gunfight waiting to see who emerged the victor.

He slid into the bushes, swallowing a groan at the
pain. He had never been so frightened. He couldn't let
them die. He had promised Cameron he would protect
them, damn it.

To his vast relief, Shumway must not have been

thinking straight, or he would have guessed Cale couldn't shoot at the SUV for fear of hitting Megan or the kids and would have used the vehicle for cover.

Instead, he ran around the side of the house, giving up his one advantage. Cale followed him with a hail of bullets, but he was shooting into the blind.

He was losing blood. He was certainly familiar with that edgy, light-headed feeling. He didn't want to think about the irony that he'd spent twelve years in the FBI without incident, but had been shot twice in less than three weeks.

If he survived this, he was never going to hear the end of it.

The shooting stopped momentarily—probably while the bastard shoved another clip into his gun—and he took as much advantage of the lull as he could.

"Give it up, Shumway," he yelled, crawling through the bushes. The only chance for all of them was for him to get close enough for a clear shot. "You planning to kill all of us?"

"I don't want to," came the muffled response. The panic came through loud and clear in his voice. "But I don't have any choice here."

The desperation chilled him. "What kind of shit do you think you're going to bring down on yourself by killing an FBI agent, a widow and two little kids? The whole country will be looking for you. You won't be able to hide anywhere, not even in the deepest, darkest mine."

There was a pause. "Nobody will know it's me," he said, though the panic ran through his voice like a vein of black coal in bedrock. "Who's going to suspect me? I'm a respected member of the community, a business owner on the town council. I've got a completely clean record."

Cale risked a glance to the car and saw Megan had shoved both children down between the seats. She raised her head above the backseat and he saw her holding her cell phone. Good. She must be calling reinforcements.

"Cameron already told the sheriff everything he saw inside that mine," Cale said, trying to buy time and lull the other man into making a mistake. "We know you killed Wally Simon, Shumway. It's only a matter of time before the sheriff comes for you. We all turn up dead and he's going to know right where to look."

"You're lying!"

"Am I?"

In answer, Shumway fired again. This shot went wild, and he heard a shattering of glass and another muffled scream. Cold dread gripped his gut and with a last burst of energy, he slithered through the bushes and rounded the corner until they were facing each other, just a few yards apart, so close he could see the sweat dripping from the other man's mustache.

"It's over, Wayne," he growled, his SIG Sauer trained between the bastard's eyes. "Drop your weapon *now!*"

Locked in a stalemate, they stood for maybe ten seconds. Cale didn't know how it would have ended if they hadn't suddenly heard the sound of sirens wailing through the night.

Distracted, Wayne shifted his gaze briefly toward the sound, but that tiny window of opportunity was all the time Cale needed.

Cale lunged with his last burst of rage and energy, bringing his elbow up to connect with Shumway's nose so hard that Shumway's head whipped back and his gun flew harmlessly into the air.

While he was still reeling from that blow, Cale brought his weapon down hard against his temple and Shumway crumpled to the ground, instantly unconscious.

Cale slid down, fought back nausea and pain, then drew in a ragged breath and yanked out his Flex-Cufs. Shumway didn't stir while he cuffed his arms and legs.

By the time he was done, he could feel the world turning gray. Damn it. He couldn't lose it, not now.

He dragged himself to Megan's car, terrified of what he might find there as his mind flashed grim images of that cabin in the mountains and those tiny bloody bodies he had found inside.

Megan and the kids had to be safe. They *had* to be. He couldn't bear any other alternative. He yanked open the door and felt his knees go weak when he found her in the backseat with a scared, sobbing child in each arm.

They were safe. They were safe.

"It's okay," he murmured, from what sounded like a thousand miles away. "Everybody's okay."

It was the last thing he remembered.

Megan watched in horror as one moment Cale offered them a reassuring grin through the shattered window, the next he tumbled to the concrete of her driveway.

For an instant she couldn't move, stunned and not quite sure what was happening. Her children still trembled in her arms, but she shifted Hailey to Cameron's arms.

"What's wrong with Agent Davis?" Cam asked.

"I'm not sure," she said grimly. "The sheriff will be here in a moment, though. Everything will be fine."

She opened the door and slid out and the moment she had a clear view of him, she knew exactly why he had passed out. She couldn't exactly miss the bullet hole in his leg.

Oh, dear heavens. He'd been shot!

Even in the hazy twilight, she could see blood everywhere, soaking the thigh of his left pant leg and already pooling on the concrete.

So much blood. She hadn't seen it, hadn't even guessed that he'd been injured. It had all happened so fast—she had been focused on the madman trying to break into her car when suddenly Shumway had whirled and fired.

It must have been in that moment. She had turned in time to see Caleb drop to the porch but she assumed he was just ducking out of the way of the gunfire.

That was at least six or seven minutes ago. During the shootout, he must have been fighting incredible pain. How in heaven's name had he managed to subdue and restrain Wayne, all with this terrible gaping hole in his leg?

She didn't take time to figure it out, knowing that with every passing moment, more of his precious lifeblood dripped away. With some vague idea of stopping the bleeding, she whipped off her jacket and folded it up to apply pressure to his wound just as the first flashing lights appeared at the edge of her driveway.

The police vehicle was immediately joined by three or four more screaming rescue vehicles. She sobbed with relief as Daniel Galvez rushed to her with his gun drawn, looking hard and dangerous.

"Where's Shumway?" he demanded.

She pointed to the crumpled form in the shadows of the garage. When Daniel realized Wayne was unconscious and restrained, he hurried to her side, ordering his deputies to call for an ambulance.

"Don't let him die," Megan begged as others came to offer first aid. "Please don't let him die."

She didn't realize she was crying until a hand reached up to wipe at her tears. She looked down and found polar-blue eyes looking up at her, despite the haze of pain in them.

"Don't cry, Megan. Not for me."

She leaned into his hand and covered his fingers with hers, holding them against her cheek for only a moment before she turned back to applying pressure on his injury.

She drew in a breath, fighting hard for control. "How many times are you going to risk your life for us, Caleb?"

He gave her a half-smile that seemed to stab straight to her heart.

"As many as it takes, I guess," he murmured, then closed his eyes and left her with the devastating realization that she deeply, completely, irrevocably loved this man.

"I'm sorry I've caused so much trouble."

Megan dropped a stitch at the small voice. She looked up from her knitting to find Cameron in his pajamas standing just outside the pool of light in the small alcove on the landing.

The last emergency worker had left an hour ago. Though she wanted desperately to rush after Cale, she knew she couldn't drag her traumatized children through more stress. They needed sleep and they needed the stability of their own beds, not to sit in a waiting room all night long.

She had to content herself with the phone call she had made fifteen minutes earlier to the clinic. Lauren hadn't been able to tell her anything because of privacy laws but she had handed the phone to Gage McKinnon, who had told her Cale was stable, alert, and already trying to escape his hospital bed.

Megan set aside her knitting and her worries for Cale to focus on her son. "Honey, this isn't your fault," she assured him, pulling him into a comforting embrace.

"If I hadn't gone inside that mine, none of this would have happened. Agent Davis wouldn't have been shot."

She closed her eyes, her stomach clenching again at the memory of all that blood. Instead of dwelling on that, she pressed her cheek against Cameron's, marveling that he was here in her arms, thanks to a man who now lay in a hospital bed.

"Don't blame yourself, sweetheart. You know you made a mistake going into the mine. We've already talked about that and we don't need to go over it again and again. But whatever your wrong decisions, you certainly didn't make Wayne Shumway shoot Agent Davis. He did that all on his own to cover up the terrible thing he did inside the mine."

"Agent Davis saved us, didn't he?" Cameron said, and she winced at the new note of hero worship in his voice. "He protected us, just like he said he would."

She kissed the top of Cam's blond head, her heart aching. "Aren't we lucky he was here?"

Not for long though. Soon he would be returning to Salt Lake and his job and the life he had there. Because of her base and miserable cowardice, she had ensured he would have no reason to stay.

"You need to get some rest," she told her son. "Come on. I'll tuck you back into bed."

She took his hand and led him to his room, where she settled him under his comforter and kissed his cheek.

"Will you leave the closet light on again?" he asked in a small voice. She wondered how long he would need that reassurance that he wasn't trapped in the dark.

"Of course," she murmured. She switched it on. As she turned to go, she caught sight of Rick's image gazing back at her from the shrine above Cameron's bed, his mouth military-solemn but those eyes she had loved dancing with so much life.

The crushing pain wasn't there anymore when she looked at his handsome features. She would always grieve for him and what they had lost. But as she gazed at that picture, she was conscious of a slow, healing peace seeping into her heart.

The loss of him had nearly killed her. But she had survived. In that moment, standing in her son's bedroom, she knew she wouldn't have traded the years of joy with Rick for anything, even if she had known about the pain in store for her from the beginning.

She shifted her gaze to Cameron, already snuggling into his pillows. That was why. Without Rick, she wouldn't have this wonderful, courageous boy, or his little sister sprawled out on her bed in the other room.

Her life would have been dry, colorless. An empty, withered wasteland.

She hadn't a tenth of her son's courage. She thought she wanted to hide away from life, from anything that threatened the safe world she had carved out for herself and her children—a safe world that had turned out to be only a chimera with no substance whatsoever.

By continuing to push Caleb away, she was ensuring that—in theory, at least—she wouldn't hurt any worse than she did right now.

In the years to come, she might be lonely and she might yearn for his arms, his smile, his strength. But she wouldn't know the gut-wrenching pain of having loved and been loved in return and then losing it all.

She thought that was what she wanted, what she needed to survive. But as she stood in her son's darkened bedroom, her hand on the light switch to his closet, she realized that by closing the door to her heart so firmly against Cale, she *was* cutting off the possibility of further pain. She would be safe there, huddled in the dark alone.

But she would also deprive herself of all the joy and happiness to be found in taking the risk, by stepping into the light and grabbing the chance life had offered her.

"Night, Mom," Cameron murmured from the bed, no doubt wondering why she didn't get on with it and let him sleep.

"Good night, sweetheart," she replied, her voice raw and unsteady with emotion.

After she left the room she stood in the hallway, her heart hammering hard as the truth settled over her. She couldn't let him walk away. She loved him. It washed through her heart, soothing and healing all the aching hollows, the battered edges.

Surely she could show at least as much courage as her son. Cameron had survived hours alone in the dark.

All she had to do was reach for the light.

Chapter 17

He made a lousy patient. He was surly and miserable and just wanted to be home sitting on his recliner with a beer.

Instead, he was propped up in a bed, his leg wrapped to the hilt, wearing a damn hospital gown and trying to talk his way out of another ambulance ride.

"You need surgery to take the bullet out," Lauren said as patiently as if he were some kind of three-year-old learning to use scissors for the first time. "My clinic is simply not equipped for that kind of thing. The trauma center at the University of Utah will take good care of you, I promise."

"Who knows? Your same room from last time might still be available. They might even offer some kind of frequent-flier discount," Gage piped up from the corner and Cale glared at him, not at all in the mood for humor.

The jokes at his expense had only begun, he knew.

Somebody had probably already hung a big shooting range target above his desk at the Bureau.

He didn't care, he told himself. He would do it all over again, endure everything, as long as he could keep Megan and the children safe.

"We don't have any choice here, Cale," Lauren said.

"I don't have a problem going to University Hospital," he said. "I really don't. I just don't want to go through the whole ambulance thing."

He hated being fussed over, and nobody fussed like a couple of paramedics on an hour-long ambulance transfer.

"Gage can drive me to the city since he seemed to think he had to rush right here from Park City. He owes me, since I seem to recall doing the same for him a few years back when he had two broken legs."

"And you're never going to let me forget that, are you? At least I never had two bullet holes in me at the same time."

Lauren broke in before he could form a heated reply. "I'm not sure transportation in a private vehicle is the wisest idea for you right now, Cale. I'm quite certain you would be far more comfortable stretched out in an ambulance than cramped in some backseat."

"I'll be fine," he started to insist, then he forgot why he even cared when he heard a subtle noise at the door. He shifted his gaze and, incredibly, found Megan standing in the doorway.

She looked slight and fragile and so heartbreakingly beautiful, he forgot about everything else. The pain, the fuzzy feeling from the drugs, the overwhelming fatigue. Everything faded away.

He couldn't speak for a moment. When he did, his voice sounded rough, ragged.

"Megan! What are you doing here? Where are the kids?"

A hint of color dusted her cheekbones. He wondered why but didn't have a chance to ask. "I called my sister to stay with them for a while. I...I had to check on you."

He flashed back to that moment on the hard concrete of her driveway when he had blinked back to consciousness to find her crying over him and trying to staunch the bleeding from his wound.

Suddenly all the discomfort and the inconvenience and the sheer misery of finding himself in a damn hospital bed again so soon seemed inconsequential.

She was here and she was safe, and that was the only thing he cared about.

He couldn't stop staring at her as wild yearning thrummed inside him. He wanted her in his arms at that moment worse than he had ever craved anything in his life.

She stared back at him, her eyes wide and full of some emotion he couldn't identify. It was corny, but for a moment it felt as if they were the only two people in the room. Gage and Lauren and the IV in his arm and the clinical surroundings—everything else seemed to disappear, leaving just the two of them.

"How are you?" she asked softly.

"Fine," he answered, not trusting himself to say more, not when they had an interested audience. Right now, wonderful. He wanted to think it was the drugs in his system but he was pretty certain it was only Megan.

McKinnon could be a pain in the neck sometimes and seemed to think Cale needed a constant babysitter, but he occasionally showed moments of rare perception. Cale decided he owed him big-time when he rose and headed for the door.

"Uh, Doc, let's go take a look at my SUV and see if we can figure out how to fit a stubborn idiot with a hole in his leg into it. Maybe if I take him to the trauma center, I can make sure he doesn't get shot at again on the way."

A moment later, they were gone. Cale could have kissed his partner when he closed the door behind him with one last amused look at the two of them.

Okay, he didn't really want to kiss Gage. He wanted to kiss Megan.

To his great disappointment, she didn't come any closer, though, and he was stuck in this damn hospital bed, hungry to touch her.

"You're leaving," she murmured.

He made a face. "Yeah. Apparently I need surgery and Lauren can't do it here. She's sending me on to the University of Utah trauma center."

"Oh." Her eyes were a dark, distressed green. "I'm so sorry you were hurt again, Cale."

"You and the kids are safe. That's the important thing. And Wayne Shumway is behind bars. He's confessed everything to the sheriff. The meth lab, the Simon murder. All of it. Once they throw in a charge of shooting an FBI officer, he won't be going anywhere for a long, long time."

Her shoulders trembled once, then twice, and he couldn't stand it anymore.

"Come here," he ordered softly.

She paused for only an instant and then she rushed to his side, throwing her arms tightly around him. He buried his face in her sweet-smelling neck and decided if he had to take a bullet, this was not a bad side benefit. Not bad at all.

She sniffed once or twice, and he shifted so he could see her face. "I thought I told you not to cry over me," he said hoarsely.

"I can't help it. If you would learn to stay out of trouble, I wouldn't have to blubber all over you."

He laughed a little in response to her tart tone, feeling better than he had since the moment he walked out onto her porch two hours earlier.

Her eyes grew haunted. "I was so frightened. When the shooting started, all I could think was that you were out there right in the middle of it, completely unprotected. The children were crying and I couldn't even think straight enough to call 911 until it was almost over."

She looked so distressed, so utterly devastated, he couldn't help himself. He stopped her words with the only method available to him. He tilted his head and captured her mouth with his and kissed her, thoroughly and effectively.

She froze for just an instant, and then she kissed him back with an enthusiasm that made him completely forget about the bullet still lodged in his thigh.

He couldn't believe she was here in his arms again. When she sent him away that morning and told him she wouldn't let herself care about him because of her past, he had tried to tell himself he wouldn't push her. He understood her feelings—she had endured great pain when her husband died and she was in no hurry to go through that again.

He had made up his mind he would be noble and self-sacrificing and respect her decision, even if it meant he would ache for her the rest of his life.

To hell with that.

Right now, with her in his arms, he knew he couldn't do it. He couldn't walk away from her and Cameron and Hailey. He needed them in his life, like he needed air and water and sunlight.

He would just have to do everything he could to convince her to take a chance on the two of them.

The alternative was just too miserable to contemplate.

She pulled away after a moment, looking rumpled and sexy, and he was gratified to see she was breathing raggedly. Good, since he felt as if he had just climbed Denali.

"I don't think Lauren will be very happy with you for agitating her patient," he murmured.

She blinked. "I...I'm sorry."

He had to laugh. "I'm not. You're better medicine than anything the good doctor can shoot into my veins."

Her flushed features turned even rosier and to his great disappointment, she slid away from him to stand just out of reach.

"Where will you go when you get out of the hospital?" she asked after a moment.

"I don't know," he answered, baffled by the question and frustrated at the barriers he was afraid she was putting up between them again. "I haven't given it much thought. Back to my house in the Avenues, I guess."

"Alone? You can't possibly!"

"Right now I'm just trying to figure out how I can wiggle out of another ambulance ride and get through a day or two in the hospital. I'm sure I'll come up with something when they let me out."

She took in a deep breath. "Will you...can I persuade you to let me bring you back to Moose Springs after your surgery so the children and I can care for you while you're recuperating?"

She went on without giving him a chance to respond past his initial shock at the offer.

"It will be noisy and chaotic and probably not at all restful. Cameron will probably talk your ear off and Hailey will no doubt want you to play with her Barbies. Or her rat, which is worse. You'll probably be bored out of your mind and sick of us after five minutes. But it would mean a great deal to me—to me and the children—if you would let us help you."

He hated people hovering over him. But somehow the idea of recuperating under the care of Megan and the children seemed close to paradise.

He could watch baseball and talk climbing with Cameron, could listen to Hailey read to him in that soft, sweet voice, could spend hours with Megan by his side, her knitting in her lap and her quiet grace and dignity warming the cold hollows in his heart.

He wanted that picture, wanted it with a fierce ache in his chest—until he remembered the scene in her kitchen that morning and her utter conviction when she told him he wasn't the kind of man she wanted.

He couldn't spend a week or so in her house falling deeper and deeper in love with her and her children, not if she planned to slam the door to anything more between them.

"I don't think that's such a great idea."

She gazed at him, and he saw quick hurt flash in her eyes before she blinked it away. "I see. Of course. As I said, with the children underfoot, it would be noisy and hectic. Not the best conditions to recover from an injury. It was foolish to suggest it."

Color climbed her cheekbones, and she suddenly looked miserably awkward.

"It's not that," Cale said. "The kids are wonderful. I already love them. You have to know that."

"Then what?"

"I can't do this with you."

"Do…do what?"

"I don't want your gratitude or some misplaced sense of obligation. Haven't you figured that out by now?"

"Cale—"

"It's already going to kill me to leave you. I'm just a man, Megan. I can only take so much. The more time I spend with you and the kids, the more it's going to rip my heart out when you make me say goodbye."

She was quiet for several seconds, the only sound in the room the quiet whoosh of the IV pump. She looked away from him, apparently fascinated by something on the floor. When she lifted her eyes to meet his gaze, there was a softness in them that hadn't been there, a vulnerability that took his breath away.

"What if…what if I don't want you to say goodbye?"

Her words hung in the air between them. He was afraid he hadn't heard them right, that somehow the combination of painkillers and Megan-induced endorphins pumping through him was messing somehow with his head.

He straightened as much as he could, cursing the

damn hospital bed. He would feel far better having this conversation when he was standing on two feet, when he could reach for her without having to beg.

"You said you didn't want this," he said warily. "You said if you would ever consider loving someone again, he would be a different man than I can ever be."

"I've said a lot of stupid things, haven't I?"

Wild hope beat in his chest, a sweet joy he had never known before, had never imagined was possible. It struggled to break free and he wanted to give it wings and let it cleanse away all the bitterness he had lived with for too long.

But lingering doubt remained. He couldn't change for her, become someone solid and safe. It would destroy both of them.

"I need my job, Megan. I wish I could tell you I would walk away from it for you, but I can't. Sometimes I hate it and hate what I have to deal with. But what I do is important and makes a difference in the world. I can't change that."

He caught his breath when she returned to his side and reached out to caress his cheek.

"Oh, Cale. I don't want you to change. I know who you are. What you are. You're a good, decent man who cares deeply about others. You've risked your life for me and my children, again and again. I love that core of strength and honor about you."

He reached for her, amazed and humbled by this incredible gift fate had bestowed on him. He kissed her fiercely, wondering how he had ever thought he was content with his life. Everything before her seemed cold and barren and empty.

"I love you, Megan. Crazy, isn't it, after such a short time. But I do. I love you and I love your children."

She was crying again, he saw with some consternation. He kissed away the tears trickling down her cheeks and was rewarded with a brilliant smile that arrowed straight to his heart.

"Does this mean you'll let us bring you back here to heal when you're out of the hospital?"

"I'm a grumpy patient," he warned. "You and the kids might be sick of me after a day."

She laughed softly and he was stunned by the depth of emotion in those green eyes, by the love and the joy he saw there.

"I doubt that." She sent him a sidelong glance. "Anyway, I'm a mother. I'm really good at kissing people and making them feel better."

Heat shot through him and he had to fight down a groan of anticipation.

She smiled, and in her eyes he saw a future stretching out ahead of them like a climb he couldn't wait to tackle, full of challenges and triumphs and wonder.

There would be hard stretches along the way, he knew. Every good climb had them. But once they reached the top, the incredible view would be worth it.

"I can't wait," he murmured.

She touched his cheek again with that aching tenderness. "Neither can I, Caleb. Neither can I."

* * * * *

Chapter 1

There was something about a parking structure that always made her feel vulnerable. In broad daylight she found them confusing, and most of the time she had too many other things on her mind. Squeezing in that extra piece of information about where she had left her vehicle sometimes created a mental meltdown.

At night, when there were fewer vehicles housed within this particular parking garage, she felt exposed, helpless. And feelings of déjà vu haunted her. It was a completely irrational reaction and as a physician, she was the first to acknowledge this. But still…

Wanting to run, she moved slowly. She retraced steps she'd taken thirteen hours ago when her day at Patience Memorial Hospital had begun. The lighting down on this level was poor, as one of the bulbs was out, and the air felt heavy and clammy, much like the day had been.

Typical New York City early autumn weather, she thought. She picked up her pace, making her way toward where she thought she remembered leaving her car, a small, vintage Toyota.

Dr. Sasha Pulaski stripped off her sweater and slung it over her arm, stifling a yawn. The sound of her heels echoed back to her. If she was lucky, she could be sound asleep in less than an hour. Never mind food, she thought. All she wanted was to commune with her pillow and a flat surface—any flat surface—for about six hours.

Not too much to ask, she thought. Unless you were an intern. Mercifully, those days were behind her, but still in front of her two youngest sisters. Five doctors and almost-doctors in one family. Not bad for the offspring of two struggling immigrants who had come into this country with nothing more than the clothes on their backs. She knew that her parents were both proud enough to burst.

A strange, popping noise sounded in the distance. Instantly Sasha stiffened, listening. Holding her breath. Memories suddenly assaulted her.

One hand was clenched at her side, and the other held tightly to the purse strap slung over her shoulder. She willed herself to relax. More than likely, it was just someone from the hospital getting into his car and going home. Or maybe it was one of the security guards, accidentally stepping on something on the ground.

In the past six months, several people had been robbed in and around the structure, and as a result the hospital had beefed up security. There was supposed to be at least one guard making the rounds at all times. That didn't make her feel all that safe. The hairs at the back of her neck stood at attention.

As she rounded the corner, heading toward where she might have left her vehicle, Sasha dug into her purse. Not for her keys, but for the comforting cylindrical shape of the small can of mace her father, Josef Pulaski, a retired NYPD police officer, insisted that she and her sisters carry with them at all times. Her fingers tightened around the small dispenser just as she saw a short, squat man up ahead. He had a mop of white hair, a kindly face and, even in his uniform, looked as if he could be a stand-in for a mall Santa Claus.

The security guard, she thought in relief, her fingers growing lax. She'd seen him around and even exchanged a few words with him on occasion. He was retired, with no family. Being a guard gave him something to do, a reason to get up each day.

The next moment, her relief began to slip away. The guard was looking down at something on the ground. There was a deep frown on his face and his body was rigid, as if frozen in place.

Sasha picked up her pace. "Mr. Stevens?" she called out. "Is something wrong?"

His head jerked in her direction. He seemed startled to see her. Or was that horror on his face?

Before she could ask him any more questions, Sasha saw what had robbed him of his speech. There was the body of a woman lying beside a car. Blood pooled beneath her head, streaming toward her frayed tan trench coat. A look of surprise was forever frozen on her pretty, bronze features.

Recognition was immediate. A scream, wide and thick, lodged itself in Sasha's throat as she struggled not to release it.

Angela. One of her colleagues.

She'd talked to Angela a little more than two hours ago. Terror vibrated through Sasha's very being.

How?

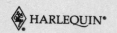

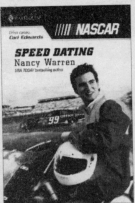

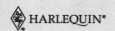
HARLEQUIN®

EVERLASTING LOVE™

Every great love has a story to tell™

Save $1.00 off

**the purchase of
any Harlequin
Everlasting Love novel**

Coupon valid from January 1, 2007
until April 30, 2007.

Valid at retail outlets in the U.S. only.
Limit one coupon per customer.

5 65373 00076 2   (8100) 0 11302

HEUSCPN0407

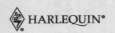

HARLEQUIN®

EVERLASTING LOVE™

Every great love has a story to tell™

EVERLASTING LOVE

Fall from Grace

Kristi Gold

Save $1.⁰⁰ off

the purchase of
any Harlequin
Everlasting Love novel

Coupon valid from January 1, 2007
until April 30, 2007.

Valid at retail outlets in Canada only.
Limit one coupon per customer.

RETAILER: Harlequin Enterprises Limited will pay the face value of this coupon plus
10.25¢ if submitted by the customer for this product only. Any other use constitutes
fraud. Coupon is nonassignable. Void if taxed, prohibited or restricted by law.
Consumer must pay any government taxes. Void if copied. Nielsen Clearing House
customers submit coupons and proof of sales to: Harlequin Enterprises Ltd. P.O.
Box 3000, Saint John, N.B. E2L 4L3. Non–NCH retailer—for reimbursement submit
coupons and proof of sales directly to: Harlequin Enterprises Ltd., Retail Marketing
Department, 225 Duncan Mill Rd., Don Mills, Ontario M3B 3K9, Canada. Valid in
Canada only. ® is a trademark of Harlequin Enterprises Ltd. Trademarks marked with
® are registered in the United States and/or other countries.

52607370

HECDNCPN0407